I0684072

Erotica Short Stories,
vol.22

7 Explicit Stories In 1

Just Plain Bob

What I Want To Do To Her

WARNING

This book contains sexually explicit scenes and adult language. It may be considered offensive to some readers. This book is for sale to adults ONLY.

Please store your files wisely where they cannot be accessed by underage readers.

* * * * * * * * * * * * * * * * * *

WANT FREE COPIES OF MY BOOKS?
Just visit my blog and download free copies of my books:
awesomeauthors.org/justplainbob

About the Publisher

4Fun Publishing, a member of **BLVNP Incorporated**, 340 S. Lemon #6200, Walnut CA 91789, info@blvnp.com / legal@blvnp.com
NOTE: Due to the highly emotional reaction of some people to works of erotic fiction, any email sent to the above address that contains foul language or religious references is automatically deleted by our anti-spam software and will not be seen. All other communications are welcome.

DISCLAIMER

Erotica Short Stories, Vol. 22

What I Want To Do To Her

7 Explicit Stories In 1

By: Just Plain Bob

© **Just Plain Bob 2015**
ISBN: 978-1-68030-365-0

Table of Contents

Bev's Night Out

Barb, my secretary, stuck her head in the door and said, "Your wife is on line 2."

I gave her a little wave to indicate that I'd heard her, finished adding the column of numbers I was working on and then picked up the phone.

"Hey, sweetie, what's up?"

"Just wanted to remind you that I'm going out with Julie after work for dinner and a couple of drinks. I left your dinner in the fridge covered in Saran Wrap. Just put it in the microwave for three minutes on high."

"Should I wait up?"

"Dirty old man!"

"Hey, I know what you are like when you come home after going out with her so don't blame me for taking advantage of it."

"I should be home by ten if you can keep your eyes open that long. Love you, baby, see you when I get home."

"Love you too, baby. Bye."

I had a scowl on my face when I hung up the phone. I did not like Julie, never had, never would. She was just a little too wild and free for my taste. She had been married three times and even though I had never been able to confirm it (Bev flatly denied it was true) I'd heard that the reason for the divorces was that Julie had been caught playing around. I didn't know if it were true or not, but there was just something about her that set my teeth on edge. But she was Bev's best friend so there wasn't much I could do about it except live with it.

Julie stood up for Bev at our wedding and since then she and Julie had gotten together at least once a week for coffee and they were constantly on the phone with each other. It hadn't been too bad there for a while, but then things changed. The big change came when Max joined the Marines and Julie (named for Bev's friend) went off to college. With nothing much except an empty nest on her hands, Bev decided to go to work. Julie got her a job where she worked and after that they went out for dinner and drinks at least once a week and at least once a week they stopped after work for drinks with their co-workers.

While I would just as soon she not spend as much time with Julie, I did enjoy the hell out of the nights she did. She would come home and fuck my brains out. I asked her once what the deal was.

"Promise you won't get angry?"

"Don't know. When you put it like that it is like telling me that there might be something to be angry about."

"Let me back up then. You know I love you, right?"

"Yes."

"You know I wouldn't do anything to screw up what we have, right?"

"Why am I suddenly starting to feel like I'm not going to like what I'm about to hear?"

"Don't be that way, baby. It isn't bad. The reason I come home horny is because when we stop for drinks we also dance and I'm a good looking girl even if I do say so myself. I get hit on a lot and when I dance with the guys who ask me I get felt up a lot. I never let it go anywhere, but it does wind me up and as soon as I get home to you you have to unwind me."

"That's the nights you stop after work, but what about the nights when it is just you and Julie?"

"Same thing. We eat and then go to a lounge for drinks. Guys start moving in on us and we let them buy us drinks and dance with us and they wind me up and you get the benefit."

She saw the look on my face and said, "Come on, baby, I've never even so much as kissed one of them. I let them buy me drinks and I dance with them. They rub up against me, cop a feel of my boobs, run their hands over my ass and I let them because I know I'm getting them hot and I'm going to leave them hanging. They all can see my rings and they try to come on to me anyway so I feel they deserve to be left with a case of blue balls. Honest, baby, I'm just having fun and you get to reap all the benefits."

It was true, I was reaping plenty of benefits. As with a lot of married couples, as we got older we had slipped into a rut. The frequency of our lovemaking had diminished to once a week and sometimes even once every two weeks. My sex life had dramatically improved once Bev had gone back to work. So I kept my dislike of Julie to myself, the same as I had for the last twenty years.

***

The next four years slid by. Max was discharged and using his benefits from the service, he went to college to earn a degree to back up what the service had taught him about computers. Julie graduated with a degree in Marketing and landed a job with a large advertising agency and Bev had moved up in her company to become the office manager. She was still stopping one a week after work with her co-workers, but Julie had gotten married again and their dinner nights slacked off to once every two weeks, but I was still reaping the benefits.

My world turned upside down on a Monday in June. I was taking a client to lunch and we were sitting at a table at Carl's Chop

House when he said:

"I wonder if today is my lucky day."

"I beg your pardon?"

"See the woman just walking over to the booth along the wall?"

I looked over and saw Julie. "Yes, I see her."

"I ran into her and another chick one night at a lounge over on Berkley. What a wild night that was. My buddy and me bought them drinks and danced a couple of dances with them and when I hit on her, all she said was, "You got a place?" The two of them were like nymphos. Me and my buddy couldn't keep up with them. They wrung us out. That one-" and he pointed at Julie, "-suggested to the other one that they go back to the lounge and see if they could pick up two more. The other one thought about it for a minute and then said no, that she had to hurry home to her husband and then she took her wedding rings out of her purse and put them on. Can I ask her to join us?"

I was saved from having to say anything because, just as Cliff was standing up to go over to Julie, her husband came in and joined her. "Oh well," Cliff said, "You snooze, you lose."

We finished our lunch and left and luckily neither Julie nor Paul noticed me. I don't know how I would have handled it if they had seen me and waved me over, especially with Cliff tagging along behind me.

After I left Cliff, I went back to my office and stared out the window as I rolled what Cliff had told me over in my mind. The other woman couldn't have been Bev. She just wasn't that kind of a woman. It had to be some other friend of Julie's. I kept telling myself that, over and over, but the thought had been planted and it started to grow. Did I really know what Bev and Julie did when they went out? No, I only knew what Bev told me which was that she cock teased and then came home horny for me to take care of. Was it true? Did she only cock tease? And was she horny because of it? Or could she possibly be horny because some guy she picked up didn't get the job done and I had to come in and finish up. I didn't know, but I knew I had to find out.

I was ashamed of myself for doubting the woman I loved, but as tight as she and Julie were, it was possible that Bev was the woman Cliff had seen with Julie. I didn't believe it, I really didn't, but a small very insistent voice in the back of my head kept saying:

"Check it out; put it to bed; eliminate the worry."

I made up my mind to follow Bev the next night she stopped with her co-workers and the next time she had dinner with Julie.

***

I knew where Bev and her co-workers stopped and so I stopped by there one Monday after work and checked the place out. There were several dark corners where I could sit and barely be noticed. The question was where would Bev and her friends sit? Figuring that there would be at least six of them, I eliminated the booths. Bev said they danced a lot so I thought they would probably sit as close to the dance floor as they could get. They would probably put at least two tables together so I looked around the room and picked what I thought would be the most likely spot.

I needed a disguise just in case Bev or Julie did look toward my dark corner. I have 20/20 vision so I bought a pair of heavy horn rimmed reading glasses and punched out the lenses. I never wore a hat so a ball cap with the bill pulled down would partially cover my face. A work shirt with a pocket protector full of pens and pencils would take the place of my normal three piece suit and complete the disguise and I could only hope and pray that it would be enough. If Bev or Julie spotted me and saw through the disguise, there would be hell to pay. There wouldn't be any way I could explain it and not come out looking bad. Especially if Bev were innocent.

But I had to know! I just had to know!

Wednesday was the day that Bev and he co-workers always stopped. They got off work at 5 o'clock so at ten to five I was sitting in my dark corner waiting for Bev and her group to arrive. The night went pretty much as Bev had always described it. I say pretty much because she left out a few things when she told me what she did. Like the fact that some guys got their hands inside her blouse, some guys slid their hands down the inside of the front of her skirt (and probably her panties) and she made no move to push those hands away. She never mentioned running her hand over the bulge in their pants and rubbing it or squeezing it.

One of the things she did tell me was that she never even so much as kissed a guy and that was a flat out lie. I watched her make out with three different guys in their booths or at their tables, but there were no trips out to the parking lot. The one thing that I did see that really bothered me was that I saw her left hand was bare - she had taken her rings off. What was it Cliff had said? When it was time for the woman to go home she took her wedding rings out of her purse and put them on?

Bev was usually home by ten-thirty so at ten I began looking for an opening where I could get up without being noticed and get out of the bar so I could be home when she got there. I saw her look at her watch and she said something to Julie and the two of them got up and headed for the ladies room. I got up and left as soon as they disappeared through the bathroom door.

I was in bed when Bev got home and she was stripping off her clothes as she came through the doorway.

"Ready for me, lover? I'm really horny tonight."

I'll just bet you are, I thought to myself as I pushed the covers off me and exposed my erection.

"Dirty old man," she said as she climbed on the bed and moved into a sixty-nine with me. As her hot mouth closed on my cock, I was looking at her pussy and wondering if any of the fingers on the hands that had gone down the front of her skirt had reached it and entered it. She pushed it down at me and I began to lick and suck.

***

She didn't have dinner with Julie that week. The following Wednesday found me in my dark corner and watching again. The night was a repeat of the previous Wednesday with one exception. Bev was making out in a booth with some guy and from where I was sitting the angle was perfect for me to be able to see under the table of the booth where Bev and the guy were sitting. He had his cock out and Bev was giving him a hand job as they necked. I was watching when he erupted and I saw Bev wipe her hand on his pants leg. She brought her hand out from underneath the table, licked her fingers and then she kissed him.

It was at that instant that I knew that Bev was the woman that Cliff had seen with Julie. The previous Wednesday had been just what Bev had always said it was; drinking, dancing and some cock teasing, though more than she let on, but when she licked the guy's cum off her fingers I knew. Now all I needed was visual proof that she was fucking other men. I got up and left the bar and didn't much care if Bev or Julie recognized me at all.

I was in bed pretending to be asleep when Bev got home and when she shook me I just mumbled and kept my head on the pillow. She shook me twice more and then reached for my cock. She stroked it and it didn't respond. For the first time in twenty-five years Bev's touch did not get a response. I lay there as she fondled me and replayed in my mind the scene where she licked the guy's cum off her fingers and I wanted to smack her hand away and scream at her to get the fuck away from me. The only reason I didn't was because I had to keep my cool until I could catch her actually fucking someone. Bev finally gave up and went to sleep, leaving me to stare at the wall and think nothing but bad, bad thoughts.

The next morning at the breakfast table Bev asked, "What happened to you last night? I came home horny as a goat and looking to get some of your first class horniness medicine and I couldn't get you up."

"I wasn't feeling all that well. Something I ate didn't agree with me and after several trips to worship at the porcelain throne I took some Sominex and tried to go to sleep."

"Try and get better today, lover, because I'm having dinner with Julie tonight and you know what that means. Couple that with last night's residual and you are going to have your work cut out for you."

I was parked down the street when Bev got off work. I saw Julie get in Bev's car with her and when they drove off I followed them. Bev drove to Duke's Steak House and they parked and went inside. Duke's was just a restaurant so I knew they would be staying only long enough to eat so I parked at the back of the lot and waited for them to come back out.

They came out an hour later and I followed them across town to a place called Barney's Roadhouse. They parked and went inside and I gave them a half-hour head start and then put my disguise on. I figured that the half-hour would give them time to become interested in or involved with someone and with luck they might not notice me come in. My disguise wasn't all that good; it would work in a dark corner, but I didn't know how it would hold up away from darkness. Luck was with me when I walked in. Bev and Julie were sitting in a booth with two men and they were busy talking and never even looked my way.

I found a place where I could sit and watch them and checked my watch. Bev was usually home by ten-thirty so if anything was going to happen it should happen soon. According to Cliff they had spent over two hours in his room. If that held true for every night Bev and Julie went out together, something would have to happen in the next fifteen or twenty minutes.

Ten minutes went by and I saw Bev say something to Julie, look at her watch and then get up and head for the woman's bathroom. A minute later the guy she had been talking to got up and went towards the men's bathroom. I sat there sipping my beer waiting for them to come back when suddenly it hit me. Women always go to the bathroom in pairs, but Julie didn't get up and follow Bev. Add to that the fact that Bev left her purse on the table for Julie to watch. What woman goes to the bathroom in a bar or restaurant without taking her purse with her if only to touch up her makeup?

I got up and headed for the bathrooms. There was a long hallway with a door on each side and the two bathrooms were at the end of the hall. I checked the doors on either side of the hall and they weren't locked. I looked in both of them and found one full of beer cases and the other full of folding tables and chairs. There was no exit so Bev and the guy had to be in the bathrooms. I checked the men's first and got the surprise of my life. The man had Bev pinned against the wall and was fucking her. Her panties were lying on the floor and her skirt was bunched up around her waist. He had her ass in his hands, her arms were around his neck and her legs were wrapped around him. He was banging into her hard and I could hear little grunts each time he drove home.

There were three guys standing there watching and discussing the possibility that they could be next. Bev was moaning as the man slammed into her and the guy said:

"Here it comes, honey. I hope you got protection 'cause I ain't pulling out."

Thirty seconds later he pulled out of her and Bev slid down to the floor in front of him and she took his limp cock in her mouth and began sucking on him. I watched her use her lips and tongue on him as the three guys asked if they could be next.

"How about it, sweet cheeks? Want to pull a train?"

Bev took her mouth off him long enough to say "no" and then she went back to sucking his cock.

"Sorry, guys," the man said. "She doesn't mind putting on a show, but I guess I'm enough for her tonight."

His cock started to stiffen and Bev stood up, turned and grabbed the sink and bent forward. The man moved behind her and slid his cock into her cunt. She grunted when he slammed into her. The look on her face was one of pure lust and she was moaning, "Yes, yes, yes, yes, yes" as he pounded into her. The man nailed her steady for about five minutes and then he said:

"Second load, baby, on the way."

"Yes, yes, yes," Bev moaned as she pushed her ass back at him.

The other three watchers, aware that they weren't going to get any and figuring the show was over, finished their business and left. The man stepped back from Bev, grabbed her skirt and wiped his cock on it and then began to tuck it away. He looked at me and smirked as he said:

"Sorry, sport, the lady said I was enough for her tonight."

The punch that broke his nose came as a complete surprise to him as did the kick in the balls that followed it. As he started to double up, I grabbed him and rammed his head into the concrete block wall a couple of times before dropping him on the floor and kicking him three more times in the stones.

I turned to Bev and saw she was looking at me terrified. I took off the ball cap and fake glasses and tossed them on top of the man lying on the floor clutching at his crotch, moaning and gasping for air. I looked at Bev's left hand and saw that it was ringless.

"I probably shouldn't have been so hard on him because he

didn't know you were married, but you knew you were. I hope you have a place to stay because I can't promise you I won't hurt you if you come home."

I turned and walked out of the bathroom. As I was walking by the booth where Julie and the other guy were still sitting, I saw he had his hand inside her blouse and she was smiling at him. I took out my cell phone and snapped a picture of it and when Julie looked up I said:

"Paul will love seeing this."

Her face turned white and I left the bar and went home.

***

I haven't seen or talked to Bev since that night in the bar. She called three dozen times in the days following that night, but I wouldn't talk to her. She has called two or three times a week since then and as soon as I hear her voice I hang up. Max and Julie call me once or twice a week to try and get me to talk to their mother and I refuse just as I refuse to tell them why.

"If your mother wants to tell you she can, but I'm not saying anything about it."

I called Paul and told him I had something to send him and asked for his email address. He called me after he got the picture and asked me about it and I told him the whole sad story from the time Cliff clued me in until the night I took the picture. I heard that he tossed Julie out on her ass.

The house was too big for just me and I didn't need all the memories that came with the place so I moved out and Bev moved in until we had to sell it as part of the divorce settlement. When we closed on the sale of the house, I sent Max with my power of attorney so I would have to look at Bev.

The divorce is final tomorrow and I'll be free to get on with my life. Will I miss Bev? I already do, and as strange as it may sound I still have some love for her. You can't just turn off twenty-five of love and affection like you can hit a light switch and turn the lights off and on.

Could I have stayed with her? No. I could have handled her night out with her co-workers if it had been no worse than it had been the first night I watched. I could have done it even though it was a lot raunchier than she led me to believe, but there was no way I could have lived with the woman who let herself bc fucked in a public restroom in front of a crowd, no fucking way!

End of the 1st Story

Julie Gets Even

Nice carriage, head up high, confident walk, nice tight ass. Maybe, just maybe, he might be the one. Or one of the ones. That would be a decision to be made after the first one. And there was going to be a first one, Julie thought as she watched Don walk past her desk. She opened the center desk drawer and took out the list she had started making and added Don's name to it. She looked at her watch and then slid the list back into the drawer. She was going to have to hurry if she was going to be on time for her lunch date with her husband.

As Julie sipped her white wine and looked at the smiling face of her husband, she wondered if the reason he was so happy was because his secretary had given him a blow job this morning. Or maybe the scheming slut had dropped her drawers and had fucked him on his desk. In a way Julie was glad that Steve had decided to cheat on her. She'd only had two sexual experiences, both less than satisfying, before she had met and married Steve and she had been a faithful wife for the seven years of their union. She had spent those seven years attending "hen" parties with her friends - Avon, Tupperware, and the like - and the favorite topic of conversation always seemed to be men. Husbands and boyfriends were talked about as if they were livestock; who was good in bed and who wasn't, who ate pussy the best, who had the biggest cock, and just about everything else you could think about. Because of all those talks Julie had always wondered about other men and now thanks to Steve's infidelity her curiosity was going to be satisfied.

She had gotten off work early one night and instead of going to the bridal shower she was supposed to be going to, she decided to skip it. She drove over to Steve's office intending to take him out to dinner. She had gotten to his office building just in time to see him opening the door of his car for his secretary Marsha. Julie was just about to honk her horn to get his attention when curiosity grabbed her. When she'd reminded Steve about the shower and not to forget that she would be home late, he said that he had to work late anyway. Maybe he and Marsha were just going for a bite to eat and then hurry back to the office, but if that were the case why didn't they just go to Anton's which was just across the street. Suddenly Julie had a bad feeling about this and she decided that she was going to follow Steve and Marsha to see what they were doing. She followed them right up to the point where they turned into the parking lot at the Shangra-La Motel. And then she had sat across the street with tears in her eyes and watched as the man she loved, the man who swore that he loved her more than life itself, checked in and took Marsha to room 136. She had pulled away from the curb and headed for the nearest bar - she needed a drink.

She was sitting at a table in a dark corner of the bar, sipping a Screwdriver, when the first man approached her and offered to buy her a drink. She was so upset at what she had seen Steve doing that she almost said yes, but she really didn't like the looks of the man so she said thanks, but no thanks. When the second man had approached her two Screwdrivers later she said yes and the man joined her at her table. Five drinks later and after she had explained to John why she was sitting in the bar alone she got up to leave. John walked her to her car and when she turned to thank him he had taken her in his arms and had kissed her. At first she had been surprised and had just stood there, but when his tongue had darted into her mouth she thought "Why not?" and she had returned the kiss. When John had asked her if she would like to go some place more private she had almost said yes, but even though she was angry with Steve she was not yet ready to take that big of a step. She told John she couldn't and he had given her his phone number. He kissed Julie again, a long passionate kiss and then they had said goodnight and Julie had headed home.

As she drove home she thought about what she should do or say to Steve, but the closer she got to the house the more she thought that she should just keep quiet. By the time she pulled into her driveway she knew what she was going to do. If adultery was good enough for Steve, it would be good enough for her.

The next day at work Julie began her list. She decided to pick ten possible lovers and then select one of them to be her first experience at extra-marital sex. The first name to go on the list was John, her drinking companion of the previous night, and over the next two weeks the list grew as she evaluated friends and fellow workers. By the time she added Don's name to the list she had pretty much decided to do all ten, but she had to see how the first one would go before making that decision.

What she really wanted to do was lean over the table and slap that smile off Steve's face, but instead she took the first step in getting back at him for betraying her. After ordering lunch she casually said, "I've been asked to take part in a large project for one of our customers and it means I'll be working late two or three nights a week until the project is complete, probably in a month or two. It will be a really good opportunity for me. If I do well I might even get a raise." And no doubt, she thought to herself, you will probably find some time on those nights to spend with Marsha. She smiled to herself as she thought that she would very possibly getting the same thing that Marsha was getting and maybe even at the same time. Steve told her he was glad that her company had finally realized her worth and he told her that he knew she would do well. They finished lunch and then Julie had kissed him and headed back to work. Step one out of the way, on to step two.

Step two was to find a way to let the ten men on the list find out that under the right circumstances she could be available. She was not going to ask any one of them to be her lover, at least not the first one, so she had to entice one of the ten into making the first move. She went down the list of names trying to decide who would get to be first, but she just couldn't make up her mind. In the end she put all of the names on a piece of paper and threw the slips of paper into a hat and then she drew one out. Ted was going to be the lucky one. Now all she had to do was to get him to make the approach. Julie came up with several elaborate schemes, none of which she expected to work. She knew, given Ted's personality, that all she had to do was be blatantly suggestive, but while she did want to get back at Steve she didn't want to act like a slut or a whore to do it.

Then, in the space of thirty seconds everything changed. Her phone rang and it was Steve calling to tell her that he had to work late. Work late my ass, she thought as she slammed down the phone. The asshole is taking that slut Marsha some place to spend a couple of hours with her. She grabbed her purse and got up and headed for the elevator. Just as the elevator door was closing her boss rushed up and stopped the door and got on. He took one look at Julie and said, "I hope that it wasn't something I said or did." Julie looked at him with a confused look and he smiled at her, "You look upset and I'm just saying that I hope that I'm not the cause."

Julie gave him a small smile and said, "Not to worry, it's just my asshole husband."

"Tell you what, if you want to talk about it I'll buy you a drink."

Julie thought for a minute and the decided that she had no reason to hurry home and she said yes. By the third drink Julie had explained the reason for her rotten mood to Ron and the he asked, "What are you going to do about it?"

"I don't honestly know."

"Well, if you decide to pay him back in the same coin I volunteer."

"But you are married."

"Honey, when it comes to having sex with a beautiful, sexy woman all men are assholes. Besides, my wife has been in California for the last three weeks visiting our kids and grandkids and she probably won't be home for at least another two."

Julie gave her boss a long look; he wasn't on her list, but he was here and available right now and she was ready right then. "As a married man you would probably keep quiet about it, wouldn't you?"

Rod grinned at her, "Absolutely. I'm not the least bit interested in anything getting back to my wife."

"How would it affect our work relationship?"

"It wouldn't. I might try and get you to stay late a lot, but that would be up to you."

Julie finished her drink, set the glass down on the table and stood up, "Let's go."

Rod stood up. "We can take my car and I'll bring you back later, okay?" Julie nodded a yes and they left the bar.

Rod led Julie into his living room and she felt guilty as hell at what she was about to do. She knew that two wrongs didn't make a right, but she also knew that her pussy was wet and that she wanted to do this. Rod turned her, put his arms around her and kissed her. As Julie hesitantly kissed him back his hands began to roam her body and she felt the heat rush to her pussy. His tongue stabbed into her mouth and she grabbed it with her mouth and began to suck on it. Rod's hands were under her skirt and his fingers were rubbing her pussy through her panties. Overwhelmed by his caresses, his kisses and the wicked feeling of excitement at getting even with her husband, Julie gave in to her desires and spread her legs to give Rod better access to her pussy. Rod broke the kiss and went to his knees in front of her. He pulled her wet panties down and when Julie stepped out of them he leaned forward and buried his face in her pussy. He licked and sucked for a minute and then he stood up and led her over to the couch, sat her down and then went down on her. Rod licked and drove his tongue in her pussy and it felt so good that she raised her ass and pushed her bush up at his mouth. Rod grabbed her ass cheeks and pulled her hard against his face and as his tongue stabbed into her she had an intense orgasm.

Rod waited until the tenseness left her body and then he stood up and began to undress. Julie rolled off the couch and onto her knees and reached out to put her hand on his hard cock. Rod stepped forward and Julie opened her mouth. His cock was about the same length as her husband's but it was about twice as fat and Julie had to stretch her mouth wide in order to get the head of his cock in her mouth. Julie sucked on the plump cock head and suddenly what she wanted more than anything was to have the cock in her mouth fill her throat with hot, thick cum. She caressed Rod's balls, teased his asshole with her finger and clamped her lips tight around him and then jacked him off with her mouth. Rod gave a low moan and grabbed the back of her head. Sensing the moment she pushed her finger into his asshole and he exploded into her mouth. Julie gulped and gulped to swallow the flood, but still a dribble or two escaped and ran down her chin. When he softened she took her mouth off him and stood up to undress.

Rod picked her up and carried her into the bedroom and then he finished undressing her. He was being slow and gentle, but Julie didn't want that. She didn't want to make love; this was revenge for what Steve had done - what Julie wanted was to be fucked! She reached out and took hold of Rod's cock and pulled him to her.

"No more foreplay, just fuck me."

He pushed her back on the bed and Julie spread her legs and grabbed his cock and guided him into her pussy. Rod pushed into her hot box and began fucking her with a fast hard tempo and Julie threw her head back, closed her eyes and appreciated the pleasure that he was giving her. She felt completely filled and then she felt it - the tingle that told her she was going to climax - and she locked her legs around her lover, grabbed his ass with both hands and pulled him deep into her as her climax rocked her body. She held him tightly to her until the waves of pleasure began to recede and then she fell back and let him pound her until she felt him erupt inside her.

The two of them were lying on their backs and staring up at the ceiling when Rod said, "I could learn to like this."

Julie was quiet for a moment, thinking that she could learn to like it too and then she said, "Could you handle me and your wife and not get caught?"

Rod laughed. "Easily, sweetheart, easily."

"Let me think about it," Julie said even though she already knew she was going to say yes. She reached over and put her hand on Rod's cock. "You're not done yet, are you?"

End of the 2nd Story

Cassandra's Guy

I met Cassandra in college during my sophomore year. I'd seen her around campus since my first day as a freshman, but our paths had never crossed. One night I was at a party and there she was, surrounded by a platoon of male admirers. We made eye contact. I smiled, she looked away and I went and got myself another beer.

I was outside on the back patio catching a breath of fresh air. It was a clear night and I was looking up at the stars when a voice behind me said, "Which one do you think I should have named after me?"

I turned and saw Cassie standing there. "Whichever one is the brightest of course," I said.

She smiled at me and said, "Why haven't I met you?"

"We don't seem to travel in the same circles."

"I saw you looking at me inside. Why didn't you come over and introduce yourself?"

It was my turn to smile at her and so I gave her my biggest and brightest and said, "I can't stand crowds."

She stuck out her hand and said, "Hi, my name is Cassandra, but my friends call me either Cassie or Cass."

We talked for a bit and then I asked her out, she accepted and so began my on again, off again relationship with the woman who would one day end up as my wife.

***

Cassie and I dated off and on for about three months before deciding that we should give it a go as a steady couple. Three months into our steady relationship I arrived at Cassie's sorority house to pick her up for a planned evening out. One of her sorority sisters handed me a note that Cassie had left for me and it said that something had come up and she would call me the next day. I went out, had dinner and caught a show. After the show I decided to stop and have a drink and I went into a place just down the street from the movie house.

I was sitting at the bar sipping a Coors Lite when I heard a familiar laugh behind me. I turned and saw Cassie sitting in a booth holding hands with some guy. Somebody dropped a few quarters into the jukebox and when the music started Cassie and the guy got up to dance. He pulled her close, she tucked her head into his chest and he dropped his hand to her ass and I saw her smile as his hands moved over her ass while they swayed to the music.

I finished my beer, got up and left. I am a somewhat curious kind of guy so I drove over to the sorority house, parked and waited. Seven in the morning came and Cassie still hadn't come home.

***

I was in my apartment when Cassie called, but I let the machine pick up the call. I went out that evening and when I came home at three in the morning the machine had three more calls from Cassie on it, all of them asking me to call. I let the machine take four calls from her on Sunday and it wasn't until Monday afternoon that we connected.

I had two hours to kill before my next class and I was sitting in the student cafeteria sipping coffee and reviewing my notes from my last class when Cassie dropped into the seat across from me. I looked up at her and then back down at my notes. When I didn't say anything Cassie said, "I've been trying to reach you all weekend. Where have you been?"

"Out trying to drown my sorrows."

"That sounds pretty serious. Dare I ask?"

"I saw my girl in a bar Friday night. She was dancing real close with some guy and didn't seem to care at all when he dropped his hand to her ass and left it there. In fact, she smiled and buried her head in his chest when he did it. But even though it didn't seem to bother her, it bothered me. Hence, I've been drowning my sorrows."

"I can explain, baby."

"No, you can't, Cassie. You had a date with me and you stood me up to go out with another guy. There just isn't any good explanation for that."

I looked at my watch. "Got to go. Time for my next class," and I got up and left her sitting there.

***

Cass was sitting on my doorstep when I got home that night. "Can I come in? I'd like to talk."

I shrugged and stepped aside to let her in. I motioned for her to take a seat and then I sat down and motioned for her to go ahead.

"First off, Bob, you don't own me."

I didn't say anything, just sat and watched her.

"I know that we are going steady, but I'm young and when I meet someone I think I'd like to get to know better I'm going to want to go out with him. I'm not ready for marriage, sweetie, and I want to look around while I can. What's wrong with that?"

"Not a thing, Cass. It is the way you did it. You had a date with me. I had reservations made for dinner and I had already purchased the tickets for the movie so we wouldn't have to stand in a long line. All of that went into the toilet when you stood me up. You want to date other guys – fine – that's your choice, but make a date with another guy and then fuck over me to keep it? No fucking way, Cassie. Speaking of fucking, did you fuck him?"

"Don't be silly."

"What did you do?"

"We had dinner and then went to the bar and had some drinks and danced and then we sat in his car and talked for a while. He had me back to the sorority house by midnight."

I stood up and walked over to the door, opened it and turned to her. "Leave, Cassandra. Just get your lying ass out of here."

"I'm not lying, Bob."

"Oh yes you are, Cassandra. I was curious about you and your date so when I left the bar I drove over to the sorority house and waited for you to come home. I was still sitting there waiting for you at seven in the morning before I finally accepted the fact that you were probably in his bed and gave up waiting. Get out, Cassandra. It is bad enough that you did it to me, but I'll be fucked if I'm going to sit here and be lied to."

"Bob, I swear…"

"Out, Cassandra, just get the fuck out!"

***

Three weeks went by and one day I came home from class to find Cassie sitting on my doorstep again. She wanted to talk so I let her in. We sat down and she said, "I've missed you. I know I screwed up, honey, and I'm sorry. Not seeing you for these three weeks has made me realize that you're my guy. Can we work it out, honey? Can we put it back together?"

She was gorgeous, she was a fantastic piece of ass and I was so in love with her that I couldn't think straight when she was around so I forgave her and we got back together and in doing so I planted the seeds of what would come back later to haunt me.

***

It was four months before it happened again, but Cassie had learned. She called me on a Thursday and told me that she had met a guy who "was really cute" and she wanted to get to know him a little better and she had agreed to go out on a date with him.

"We don't have anything planned for this weekend so I told him I would go out with him Saturday. I just wanted you to know so that you don't think that I'm sneaking around behind your back."

Things were a little 'chilly' between us for the next couple of weeks, but eventually I let her persuade me that it was me she really loved and things smoothed out. Cassie did that to me six more times before we graduated and each time we ended up back together. I guess that I was pussy whipped – Cassie was that good.

***

A month before graduation (and two months after her last little "walk about") Cassie asked me when I was going to get around to asking her to marry me. I might have been pussy whipped, but I wasn't stupid.

"I hadn't planned on asking you to marry me."

Cassie sat there and looked at me with a stunned expression on her face. "What? But I thought we had something going for us. I thought that you loved me."

"I do, Cassie, but being in love doesn't automatically mean that I have to be stupid. I'm not about to marry a woman who always seems to find a really cute guy that she wants to get to know better. You have been doing that to me for as long as we have been keeping company and I love you so much that I always ended up forgiving you for it and staying with you. That was something that I could do as long as we were single, but there is no way I would put up with that if we were married and quite frankly, I don't think you will ever change."

"You can't mean that, baby. You know you are my guy. Sure I've checked out other guys, but isn't that what a girl is supposed to do? Make sure that she picks the right guy before getting married? I've looked, honey, and you're the best there is. You are my guy, baby. The search is over."

"That is what you are saying now, Cass, but I've been through this too many times now. Each time I get the "You're my guy" speech and I say okay and let it go, but two or three months later you have another cute guy that you just have to check out. I don't believe that you are ever going to change and I'm not about to get married to a woman I can't trust."

"Okay then, how about this. We live together for one year and see how it goes. I'm serious about this, honey. You're my guy and I know it so just give me a chance to prove it."

What could it hurt, I thought and besides, I really did like having her around.

***

We graduated, found jobs and set up housekeeping together. Everything seemed to be working out well for us and I began to think that maybe I was Cassie's guy after all. About six months into our arrangement the company sent me out of town for two days. The day I got back I went straight to the apartment from the airport and as I came in the front door the phone started to ring. The telephone answering machine took the call before I could get to the phone:

"Hi, Cassie, this is Daren. Hey listen, I had a great time last night and I'd like to do it again. Give me a call, okay?"

He gave his number and hung up. I dropped my bags and walked over to the machine and looked down at it. Should I erase the message and not let Cassie know that I knew or leave it and see what happened? I opted for the latter and went into the bedroom and unpacked.

When Cass got home I was in the kitchen and she came in and gave me a big hug and a kiss. "Welcome home, Tiger. It's only five-thirty, but are you ready for bed?"

"In a little while maybe. You have a message on the machine."

Cass went over and hit the PLAY button and I saw her face cloud over when she heard the message. She looked over and saw me watching her. "It isn't what you are thinking, honey."

I just stood there and looked at her while the message played out. When it was over Cassie hit the DELETE button and then came over to me and put her arms around me.

"It isn't what you think. One of the girls I work with asked me to stop after work and have a drink with her. You were gone and I didn't want to come home to an empty apartment so I said yes. While we were there she got a call from her boyfriend on her cell phone and she told him where we were and to come on over. He got there and we had a couple of drinks and then a friend of his came in, saw him and came over to join us. The four of us were sitting there talking when a band came in, set up and started to play. We had some drinks, I danced with both guys a couple of times and then I got up and left. He must have gotten my number from Sarah. Honest, honey, that's all there was to it."

I must have looked a little skeptical because she said, "Come on, baby, give me some credit for brains here. If I were doing what you are thinking, would I have given him my home phone number? No, I would not have. I would have given him my cell phone number or my number at work. Come on, baby, it's been two days now, take me to bed."

It sounded reasonable so I put it out of my mind and forgot about it. The rest of the year went by quickly and Cassie again brought up marriage and so I asked, she said yes and we tied the knot.

***

A year went by and Cassie and I were doing great. Our relationship was strong, we both had good jobs and we liked what we were doing. We had settled into a comfortable life style, bought a house, furnished it and fell into a routine. She stopped with the girls from work one night a week, usually on a Tuesday because that was the night I bowled. I played cards one night a week with my buddies, usually on a Thursday because that was the night Cassie played cards with her sorority sisters from college. The only other times she went out were the nights when I was out of town. On those nights rather than sit home alone she would have dinner with one or two of the girls she worked with. And then one evening I found out just how stupid I really was.

I came home from work just in time to see Cassie grab her purse and head for the door. "We going somewhere?"

"Not we, honey, just me."

"Where are you going?"

"I've got a date."

"You have a date?"

"Yes. Sarah introduced me to a friend of her boyfriend and he asked me out."

"You are serious? You are actually going on a date with another man? Cass, has it occurred to you that you are married now, not single and back in college?"

"It will be all right, honey, trust me," and she walked by me and out the door.

***

I was sitting up waiting when she came home at three in the morning. "Oh, you're up. I expected you to be in bed."

"Not hardly. We have some talking to do."

"Oh well, all right. Come on, we can do it while I undress," and she headed for the stairs. I followed and sat on the bed and watched while she took off her clothes.

"I want an explanation, Cassie. I thought we had a good marriage and I would like to know why you just tossed it on the trash heap."

I saw the hickey on her neck as the turtle neck sweater came off and I saw the love bites on her tits when her bra came off and I knew what I would find if I took the time to look at the crotch of her panties.

"Don't be silly, honey. I haven't thrown anything away. I'm here, aren't I? You can always trust me to come home to you."

"I can't believe the attitude you are taking. You are here, you came home, so it's all right?"

"It always has been in the past. I mean you always sulk and pout for a while – I suppose that it has to do with ego or male insecurity – but we always end up back in each other's arms. You're my guy, baby, you've always known that."

"That was different; we weren't married then."

"Oh come on, Robert. You know very well that I've been doing it since we got married and you have turned a blind eye to it."

"No, Cassie, I did not know."

"Of course you did. You know full well what I do on Tuesday nights and some Thursdays and you know what I'm doing on the nights you are out of town. I know that you like to pretend otherwise because it soothes your masculine pride, but you know that you have known."

"Have you forgotten why we lived together for a year, Cass? It was to make sure that you were through with running around on me. Why would I have done that, Cass, if your running around was something that I was willing to suffer through?"

"Baby, baby, baby. You know I was still doing it. You heard that message on the recorder and you let yourself believe what I told you even though you knew what was going on. Now come on and stop this foolishness and let's go to bed. I want you to make love to me."

"Haven't you already had enough dick tonight?"

"Don't be crude, honey. Yes, I have had sex tonight, but now I want to be made love to."

I walked over to the dresser and opened the drawer where Cassie kept her sex toys, grabbed a dildo and tossed it to her. "Here you go, Cassandra, the only lover that you'll have in this house," and I left the room.

***

I spent an hour sitting in the living room just staring at the wall and shaking with anger and then I got up and went to the spare bedroom and tried to go to sleep. I tossed and turned a lot, but I finally did manage to fall asleep. When I woke up Cassie was in bed with me, one leg over mine and an arm around me. I pulled myself away from her and she woke up.

"What are you doing here?"

"I belong here. You are my guy and I'm supposed to be with you."

"Horse shit, Cassie. After the shit you pulled on me yesterday and what you admitted to last night when you got home, this marriage is over and I don't want you anywhere near me."

"Don't be silly, honey. I love you and you know I do and I know that you love me. The fact that I need a little something different once in a while doesn't mean that I don't want to be married to you. Come on, honey, let's start the day out right. Make love to me."

"Cassie, give it up! We are through. I don't know how you got it in your head that I knew what you were doing and that I was giving you tacit approval by not bringing it up, but you are wrong. I did not know and had I known, this farce of a marriage would have been over long ago. Now just leave me the fuck alone," and I got up to take my shower and get ready to go to work.

When I came downstairs Cassie was waiting for me. "Honey, please, we need to talk."

"We talked, Cassie, we talked when you got home last night and I heard more than enough and I didn't like any of it."

I grabbed my briefcase and went to work.

***

Fortunately I was in the end stages of a project and I was able to lose myself in my work that day and not have to spend time thinking of

Cassie and our dead marriage. I had thought about it on the way to work and again on the way home and I had begun to make a mental list of the things that I was going to have to do.

Cassie wasn't home when I got there and I sat down at the kitchen table and began to write down all the things that I had come up with. Find a divorce lawyer, find a realtor to sell the house, close out all joint accounts, etc., etc., and I was debating on whether or not to cancel the life insurance policy I had on Cassie when I heard the front door open and Cassie call out, "Honey, I'm home." Big fucking deal, I thought and I went back to my list.

Cassie came into the kitchen and I looked up to see her smiling at me. "Hi, honey," and she bent to kiss me and I turned my face away from her and she frowned.

"Come on, honey, don't be like that. You know you love me. It will work out; it always has. I've thought about it all day and I think I have finally figured out what the problem is. I don't know why I didn't see it sooner; it was right there in front of me all the time. You feel left out. Well, I've taken care of that, honey."

The doorbell rang. "Here he is now. A little early, he must be eager. Come on, honey, let's go welcome our guest."

She headed off to answer the door and I just sat there shaking my head. It didn't seem to matter what I said to her or how forcefully I said it, in her mind everything was okay because she just knew that I loved her and that I knew that she loved me. I got up to go see what she was up to now.

***

She was leading a tall good looking man toward the kitchen and she said, "Bob, this is Paul. Paul, this is my husband Bob."

The man stuck his hand out; caught by surprise and not knowing what else to do I took it and we shook hands.

"Paul has been after me for about a month now so today I called him and asked him over. I know this is sudden and that you weren't expecting it, but I'm sorry about having left you out for so long and I wanted to get a quick start on making it up to you. I know that this is all new to you and you may want to ease into it. You may only want to watch the first time or two or you may want to just jump right in. There isn't any pressure, honey, just do what you want. Come on, Paul," and she took him by the hand and headed off toward the bedroom.

I just stood there and stared at her back as she walked away with Paul. I'd spent two and a half years with her in college, lived with her for a year and had been married to her for just a little over a year. After all that time you would think that I would know her pretty well, but it was now obvious that where she was concerned I really did not have a clue.

And it seemed that she didn't know me any better than I knew her. How could she possibly think that I could accept what she was doing? Where did she get the idea that just because she said she loved me and that she knew that I loved her that everything was okay? And just where in the hell had the idea that all that was wrong was that I felt left out come from? Did she really think that I was going to follow her and her lover, boyfriend or whatever he was to the bedroom?

I grabbed my coat and was headed for the door when I heard Cassie shout, "Oh Jesus yes, just like that, just like that" from the bedroom. I don't know why, but all of a sudden curiosity got the best of me and I headed for the bedroom.

Paul was lying on his back and Cassie was working her way up and down on the biggest cock I had ever seen on a human being.

"God, I've never been so full," she moaned. "I'm going to be stretched out of shape for a week."

She rocked back and forth and moved up and down and moaned in pleasure, "Oh yes, oh yes, oh god yes. Don't stop, baby, don't lose it, don't lose it, work with me, baby, work with me, stay with me, stay with meeeeeeeeeeeeeeeeeeeeeeee," and she had the strongest orgasm I'd ever seen.

Paul gripped her and rolled with her ending up on top and then he started pounding her pussy to reach his own climax. Cassie moaned and grunted as he slammed into her and just as he said, "Here it comes, baby, here it comes," Cassie had another large orgasm. Paul rested on his hands for a couple of moments and then he lifted himself off of Cassie and fell to the bed next to her.

A minute passed and then Cassie sat up and smiled at me. The she got on her hands and knees with her ass toward me.

"Come on, honey, make love to me while I get Paul hard again."

I should have turned and run screaming from the room, but I didn't. I had been fascinated by the sight of Cassie riding that huge cock and the sounds that she had made while doing it. Also, her cunt had looked like I could have put my clenched fist into it when Paul had pulled out and for some perverse reason that I couldn't understand I wanted to – no, I had to – see what it felt like to follow that huge piece of meat into her.

As I undressed I watched her put both hands around Paul's cock and lean down and take it in her mouth and I wondered if she would choke to death when it got hard. I moved up behind her and put my hands on her hips and pushed my cock into her cunt. It was hot and it was wet and it felt good, but there was no way in hell that I was ever going to be able to cum fucking her pussy – there just wasn't any friction. But my cock was hard and after being dragged into this affair I wasn't going to leave the room without cumming and Cassie's mouth was full so I went for the only other available option – her asshole.

Cassie had never liked anal sex, but that was just tough shit (pardon the pun) as far as I was concerned. I had a hard on and she only had one hole available that was tight enough to get me off and besides, I wasn't all that happy with her right then anyway. I didn't give her any advance notice; I just pulled my cum covered cock out of her pussy, lined it up with her anal rosebud and then pushed. Cassie screamed, but it wasn't all that loud because she had her mouth full of Paul's cock. I suppose I should have warned Paul so Cassie wouldn't bite off his dick, but I didn't owe him anything and he had gone after Cassie knowing that she was married.

Whatever, when I pushed in and she screamed she tried to pull her mouth off of his cock, but he grabbed her head with both hands and wouldn't let her go. It took me three or four strokes to get myself all the way into her ass and she screamed and groaned and tried to pull away from me, but I held on tight and wouldn't let her go. I had a good grip on her hips and I held on tight as I started banging away at her ass as hard as I could. Cassie's screams turned into moans and groans and she kept trying to pull away and that only made me try to fuck her harder and faster. Then, about three or four minutes into it Cassie started a long, low moan and she stopped trying to pull away. In another minute she was actually pushing back at me and the thought of her responding excited me enough to push me over the edge and I came. My cock started to go soft and I didn't want it to. I wanted to stay in Cassie's ass and from the way she was pushing back at me I think that she wanted it to.

***

But my cock didn't stay hard and when I pulled out of Cassie's ass I immediately started wondering just what the hell I was doing taking part in Cassie's sick little sexcapade. That wasn't the kind of guy I was. Why was I letting her pull me down to her level?

I saw that she had a good three inches of Paul's cock in her mouth and she was jacking him off with both hands. I shook my head in disgust and started gathering up my clothes. Cassie had Paul hard and was ready to take him on again and when she pulled her mouth off of him she saw me getting ready to leave.

"Where are you going, Bobby?"

"Anywhere away from here."

"No, honey, go and wash yourself. I want you in my mouth while Paul stuffs me again."

When I heard that I snapped! I'd had enough. I dropped my clothes on the floor and walked back over to the bed. I grabbed a handful of Cassie's hair and pushed my dirty, slimy, shit-coated cock into her mouth. "You want it clean, you fucking whore, you clean it."

I held her head with both hands and started fucking her face as Paul got up and got into position to take Cassie from behind. As soon as he pushed into her my whore of a wife gave a moan and started pushing her ass back at him. In less than a minute she was so lost in being fucked by that huge cock that she had forgotten all about how filthy my cock was and began sucking on me. I let go of her hair and stood there wondering at the sluttishness of it all. Paul was pounding away at Cassie and he looked at me. "You sure have one hot sex maniac here. I wish my wife was like her."

"You're married?"

"Yeah, to the hottest looking, coldest fish in town. I prowl because I can't get any at home."

I wondered which of us really had it the worst: Me with a wife who did too much or him with a wife who did too little. At least in his case, if she wasn't fucking him she probably wasn't out fucking everybody else. My thoughts were interrupted by Cassie taking her mouth off me and telling Paul that she wanted to be on top. Then she turned to me and said, "I want you in my ass, honey. I want Paul in my pussy and you in my ass at the same time."

Good God, I thought, just how depraved is this woman that I

married? Still, the idea of being in her ass again did appeal to me so I got on the bed and moved behind her. It wasn't as easy to slide into her the second time as I'd thought it would be. Paul had her cunt stretched so tight that I not only had to fight the tightness of Cassie's ass, but the fact that his super large cock was pushing up at the thin membrane separating the two chambers and taking up some of the room.

It was awkward trying to establish a rhythm with Paul and while the sensation of our two cocks rubbing together was weird on another level it was also extremely exciting. Even though our threesome had been Cassie's idea from the groans she was making I didn't think she was enjoying it all that much and that thought made me happy. In fact, it made me so happy that I started banging into her butt harder to try and add to her discomfort. Banging into her harder however caused me to climax faster and it wasn't long before I sent my second load of the night to join the first in Cassie's ass.

As soon as my limp cock was out of Cassie's ass and I was off the bed Paul rolled her over and got on top. Cassie's legs came up and locked around him and I gathered up my clothes and left the room while Paul pounded into her and she cried out in pleasure.

***

In the spare bedroom I laid on the bed and stared up at the ceiling and wondered why I hadn't stuck to my guns when I told Cassie that I hadn't planned on asking her to marry me.

I knew then what she was so why had I let her convince me that marriage would change her? Was she right when she said I knew all along what she was doing? Had I been pushing the knowledge deep down into my subconscious where it would remain hidden so I wouldn't have to confront her? Was she right when she said that it didn't matter because I knew that she loved me and that I knew that I loved her? Did I really?

And what about our night? The ease with which Cassie had

handled it told me that it hadn't been the first time that she had been with more than one man. As for the threesome itself, part of me was disgusted with myself for having done it and lowering myself to her level, but part of me had loved seeing that huge cock of Paul's being swallowed by Cassie's little pussy. And what about my not wanting to leave her ass after I had come in it – my wishing that my cock would stay hard so I could stay there? I fell asleep to the sounds of Cassie begging Paul to fuck her and with a headful of questions that I didn't have any answers for.

***

I woke up the next morning with Cassie wrapped around me. As soon as I stirred I felt her hand slide down my body and take hold of my cock.

"Good morning, my love," she said. "How are you feeling this morning?"

"Embarrassed."

"About what?"

"Taking part in what you did last night. I would feel better about myself if I had just taken my coat and left."

"Don't say that, honey. You had a good time, I know you did."

"No, Cassandra. What I had was an overwhelming curiosity to see if you could actually take the huge thing that Paul had without hurting yourself. Everything else happened because I had to stick around to see."

Cassie giggled. "He was awesome, wasn't he? I had no idea that he was so well equipped when I agreed to see him."

"Yeah, well you certainly seemed taken with him last night. You didn't even notice when I left the room. There is a bright side to this I suppose. He can be your fulltime boyfriend when I move out."

"Damn it, honey, stop talking like that. You are my guy and I'm not letting you go. As far as Paul is concerned he was a one-night stand. He was great and I would love to be able to play with him three or four times a week, but I can't do that because it wouldn't be fair to you."

"What the hell does that mean?"

"It means that if I kept seeing him you would never be able to make love to me again because you wouldn't fit any more. As it is you will probably have to settle for my ass and blow jobs for the next few days to give me time to tighten up."

"What the fuck is wrong with you, Cassandra? We are through!! The marriage is over and we are through, through, through!!!"

"Don't be silly, Robert. If we were through my hand would be holding a limp dick right now instead of a rock hard cock."

I hadn't been paying attention to what her hand was doing while we were talking, but she was right, I was hard, and I didn't fight her off when she lowered her head and took me in her mouth.

Neither did I run from the room when got on her hands and knees and said, "Go slow, honey, I have to get used to this ass thing."

The unfaithful cunt knew me better than I knew myself. As I slid my cock into her hot, tight ass she moaned and laid her head down on a pillow. About two minutes into the ass fuck she said, "Maybe once a month. What do you think, honey, once a month?"

"Once a month what?"

"Maybe I could see Paul once a month. Would that be okay?"

Fucking bitch I though as I pounded my cock into her tight ass. I guessed I'd better get used to using it.

End of the 3rd Story

Brenda and David

It is always a blow to your ego when you find out that your wife is fucking another man. Once you get past the, "Unfaithful fucking whore" and the "I'll kill the mother fucker" stage you are left with all the questions of why. What did I do or not do that made her do what she did? What was I lacking? What did he have that I didn't? More energy and staying power? A bigger dick? A longer and more talented tongue? Maybe she just didn't like me anymore or maybe I had a bad case of body odor. I didn't know and I wasn't going to ask. I did not intend to let Brenda know that I knew, at least not until I was ready and had all my ducks lined up in a row.

***

I would guess that it started when Brenda and I went up to Vail to spend a weekend at the resort to celebrate our tenth wedding anniversary. Saturday night we went out for drinks and dancing and on the way into the club I tripped and twisted my ankle. I hobbled to our table and sat down and ordered drinks, but obviously, at least for me, dancing was out.

Brenda sat at the table and watched the dance floor and her body swayed in time to the music. After we had been there an hour a young man came over from where he had been sitting at the bar and asked Brenda if she would like to dance. She looked at me and I told her to go ahead and enjoy herself. The two of them went out on the floor and stayed there until the end of the set. When the band took their break Brenda brought the young man back to the table, introduced me to David and then she asked him to join us. David and Brenda danced several more times that night and I noticed that on some of the slow numbers that they danced real close to each other, but I didn't think anything of it; why should I, I was right there.

The next day I left Brenda at the pool and I drove over to the clinic at Avon and had the ankle looked at. They x-rayed it and found nothing broken and then wrapped it in an Ace bandage. When I got back from the clinic I went out to the pool and saw David rubbing sun tan lotion on Brenda's back and legs. Again, I didn't think anything about it at the time.

The weekend over we headed on home and on Monday it was back to the old grindstone for me. When you own your own business there isn't a lot of free time. You put in a lot of hours to try and make the business go and grow and I'm afraid that I left Brenda at home a lot. She never complained and while I did spend a lot of time at work I never neglected her. I made sure that our love life didn't go stale. I made love to her four or five times a week and I made sure that she knew that she was special to me.

***

It was two weeks after our weekend in Vail. I was busy at the office when all the power went out. I called the electric company and found out that a truck had hit a pole and the wires were down and the transformer had shorted out. I was told that it would be several hours before power was restored so I locked the place up and headed on home.

I hadn't taken two steps into the house when I heard Brenda moaning from the direction of the bedroom. It wasn't a 'hurt' type moan, but a sexual one. Thinking that she was working on herself with either her fingers or one of her toys I smiled and headed for the room and then stopped dead in my tracks as I saw a man's trousers and a man's pair of shoes on the kitchen floor. A few feet away I saw Brenda's nightgown on the floor. I took several cautious steps down the hall toward the bedroom and I heard Brenda moan again.

"I'll be your slut, baby. I'll do anything you want, whenever you want, just keep fucking me like you did the first time."

"Oh I will, sweet stuff, but you have to help me get it up again."

"Bring it here, lover."

Anger was building up in me, but I have never been one to act rashly and I decided to see if I couldn't find out more of what was happening before doing anything. I quietly moved back the way I had come and went out into the garage. I got an inspection mirror from my toolbox and headed back toward the bedroom. I got down on my knees and slid the mirror past the doorframe and in it I saw that Brenda and the man were facing away from the door. I got up and quickly moved to the spare bedroom which was just across the hall from the master bedroom. I slipped inside and left the door opened just a crack so I could see across the hall.

Brenda was on her knees sucking her lover's cock while one had cupped and caressed his balls. The man's hands were kneading Brenda's tits and tweaking her nipples. Brenda's nipples are very sensitive and she moaned again, pulled her mouth off the man and got on the bed. She spread her legs, pulled her knees back as far as they would go and opened herself up for him.

"Come on, lover, fuck me again. Please, baby, hurry, I need it."

The man moved to get between Brenda's legs and for the first time I saw that it was David.

"Come on, baby, hurry," moaned Brenda and David moved forward. Brenda grabbed his cock and guided it in to her and I heard her grunt as David drove his cock home. Then he fucked her. He slammed into her hard and fast and Brenda's screams rang through the house. It seemed the more noise Brenda made the more vocal David became.

"Like it, bitch? Like my cock ramming your pussy? Tell me you are my slut. Tell me that you are going to let me fuck you from now on. Come on, you unfaithful whore; tell me whose bitch you are."

Brenda moaned, cried and answered him, "Oh god, I love it.

Fuck me, fuck me harder. I'm yours, lover, whenever you want me I'm yours. I'm your bitch, I'm yours, oh god yes, fuck me."

It was almost ten minutes before David announced that he was cumming and Brenda cried out, "Pull out, pull out, baby, don't cum in me, don't get me pregnant."

David pulled out and spit his load all over Brenda's stomach. I watched as she scooped some up with her fingers and then licked them. "Damn, lover, you taste good. I should have had you cum in my mouth."

"Next time, you delicious little slut. God but you are good pussy."

"You are pretty good yourself. I knew you would be great. I wanted to sneak off and fuck you when we were in Vail, but couldn't."

"That's okay, baby, we've found each other now and I'm looking forward to a long, long relationship."

"Can you get it up again?"

"Can you help?"

I watched the two of them go at it for another hour and a half as I plotted my revenge. I almost lost it when David got Brenda on her knees, lubed himself up with KY and then took her anal cherry. That was something that she had always refused to let me do and it took all my will power to make me stay where I was and continue watching. After David had cum in her ass Brenda got up and said she was going to shower before they did any more. David said he would join her and as soon as they were in the bathroom I quietly left the house and went back to my office.

***

The power was back on when I got back to my office and I sat down at my desk and started to make a list of things that I was going to have to do to make sure that I came out of the divorce without Brenda raping financially. For the time being the target of my wrath was going to be David. I called and made an appointment with a private detective and luckily he was able to get me in the same day. I gave him what information I had and a key to my house and then signed a form giving him permission to wire the house for video and sound.

That night when I got home Brenda was all lovey-dovey and when we went to bed she immediately went after my cock. She sucked it for a while and then we made love and then she played with it and sucked it some more until it was hard again and then she surprised me.

"Can I ask you something, honey?"

"Sure."

"I know I've always said no before, but I'm curious. I want to see what anal sex is like. Would you like to do me there?"

"You sure about that?"

"I'm sure that I want to try. I'm not at all that sure that I'll like it, but I do want to try."

"Why now, after all these years?"

"You won't laugh?"

"No, I won't laugh."

"I was reading in Cosmo about things that could put some zing back in your sex life and one of the things it said to do was to take a chance and do something that you have always been leery of trying."

"You saying that our sex life needs some zing?"

"I don't know. What do you think? The frequency is there, but where did the passion go?"

"Okay, baby, if that's what you want."

I already knew that she liked having her butt fucked since I had watched and listened as she went crazy when David stuffed his dick up her poop chute. Still, I almost broke out laughing when she told me to go easy since it was her first time. I did take it slow and easy until she started pushing her ass back at me and moaning for me to make her cum. The result was that anal sex became a regular part of our sexual repertoire.

***

A week went by and I got a call to go and see the detective. He gave me his report and a box full of audio and video tapes and told me that I had more than enough to go with. Then I gave him another job and he said it would take him about a week.

I was having a hard time figuring it out. On the surface Brenda was as loving and devoted a wife as she had ever been and I'm not sure what David was doing to cause it, but she was more passionate and demanding in bed. I was having some of the best sex of my life and had I not come home and seen her infidelity with my own eyes I would have never believed it possible. But that changed nothing. She had betrayed me and was still betraying me three and four days a week while I was at work busting my ass.

The detective called me and told me that he had what I was looking for. It was everything that there was to know about David. Where he worked, what kind of car he drove, where he went when he wasn't at work or fucking my wife, everything that could be found out about him in a week. I took the report and headed back to my office. I had several friends who owed me favors and I made some phone calls and lined up some help.

David's car was an old beater and the only insurance that he had on it was the state mandated liability insurance so one night when he got off work and found all four tires slashed he had to foot the replacement bill himself. Two nights later it wouldn't start and he had to have towed in to a shop where they discovered that someone had filled his gas tank with sugar.

Next, several of my friends went into the store where David worked and bought several hundred dollars' worth of merchandise. David's boss received an anonymous phone call that David was seen carrying stuff out of the back door of the store and putting it in his car. The boss went and looked, asked David for an explanation and all David could say was that he knew nothing about it. He was fired for theft.

He found a job working in a warehouse and the police got an anonymous phone call that David was selling drugs out of his locker at work. The police showed up with a warrant to search the premises and a sniffer dog that indicated that there was something in David's locker. When it was opened they found a little over six ounces of marijuana, enough to charge him with possession with intent to sell. His father went his bail, but two days later the police got another tip and they pulled David over and found seven ounces of weed in the trunk of his car. That time his father wouldn't go his bail.

I was sitting in the front row in the courtroom on the day he was sentenced for a year and a day and when he saw me I smiled at him and he suddenly knew why his life had turned to shit. Apparently Brenda went to see him during visiting hours and he told her about my being in court and how I had smiled at him. I could see her looking at me from time to time as if wondering when I'm going to drop the bomb on her.

***

Brenda still plays the part of the loving wife and sometimes she even seems frantic in her desire to please me and I just coast along not giving any indication that I know what she did.

Meanwhile I am quietly moving assets and making the arrangements necessary to see that she comes out of the divorce penniless and with a totally destroyed reputation. Until then I treat her like the loving wife that she hopes that I still think she is. The sex is fantastic and I'm going to miss it when she's gone, but that may not be for a little while yet. I am a very patient man and I will wait to lower the boom on her until every t is crossed and I have dotted every i.

Right now I am working on a little scenario that I'm hoping that I can make work. What I want to do is take a drive with Brenda one day and end up in front of the prison just as David is released. I'll put Brenda out of the car and a pre-positioned man will serve her with the divorce papers as I drive off and leave her there with her lover. It will take some work and some very good timing, but I'm making progress and I do have my hopes.

End of the 4th Story

Making Patty Cum

I first saw my wife-to-be when she was eighteen. There was no "love at first sight" or "I just knew she was made for me." All that was there was curiosity about why she was doing what she was doing - she was letting herself be gangbanged by seven guys who were older than she was.

I was visiting my aunt and uncle for a couple of weeks during summer vacation and one day my cousin Lou asked me if I had ever taken part in a gangbang. I told him no, but that I'd heard about them. Lou said that a guy he knew was going to get Patty Kimball down in the basement of his house and gangbang her and did I want to come along? What the hell, I was only twenty and had only just recently lost my cherry so naturally I was willing. Lou made a couple of phone calls and off we went. When we got to the friend's house Lou led me around to the back of the house, in the backdoor and then down into the basement.

Once in the basement I saw that the festivities had already started. There was a cute little redhead lying on a mattress with her skirt up around her waist and her legs up on the shoulders of a guy fucking her. There were five other boys standing around waiting for their turn and Lou and I made the total eight. The girl had her eyes closed and the only sounds she made were a series of low grunts every time the guy fucking her pushed into her.

I was standing off to the side watching and her eyes never opened until the fourth guy was fucking her and then they opened and she was looking right at me and for some reason they stayed on me the entire time he fucked her. Number five moved her onto her knees and took her from behind and another guy sat down in front of her and pushed his dick in her mouth. Like I said earlier, I had just recently lost my virginity and I had never seen a blow job, just heard about them, so I was fascinated watching her mouth move up and down on the boy's cock. Once again she glanced my way and caught me staring at her and from that point on she never took her eyes off mine.

Since Lou and I had been the last to arrive we were the last to ride the train. Lou told me to go first and as I dropped my pants the redhead's eyes stayed on me. I never felt anything like the feel of her slippery hole as I slid into her and looked down into those eyes that kept looking up at me. My first three times with a girl I had been really quick to cum, but the last time, the fourth, I had lasted almost five minutes. I hoped that I wouldn't cum too quick and humiliate myself in front of Lou's friends. I needn't have worried because for some reason I couldn't cum. I fucked the little redhead for almost ten minutes before Lou and the guys started hollering for me to hurry up and finish. The redhead, I finally remembered that her name was Patty, hissed at me:

"Ignore them. You've almost got me there, don't stop now damn it, don't stop now!"

I kept pounding at her and to my amazement she let out a loud "Oh yes, oh yes, oh God yes" and her body trembled and shook like she had a fever. I was scared that she was hurt and I started to pull away from her, but she grabbed my ass and pulled me back down and cried in my ear, "Fuck me, damn you, fuck me." In the back I heard one of the guys say:

"God damn. He made her cum. Two years now I've been fucking her and I never seen her cum."

In my ear Patty was panting, "Fuck me, fuck me, don't you dare stop fucking me," and I pumped as hard as I could trying to get myself off. I felt the rush coming and I looked down to see her staring up at me with a strange look on her face and her eyes told me that she knew I was getting ready to let go and she started moaning, "Please, please, please" and just as I shot my load her body shook again and again and she cried "Oh god yes." I collapsed on her and Lou's hands grabbed me and started to pull me up, but Patty's hands were trying to pull me back down. Lou thought I was resisting him and he said:

"Damn it! Get off. I want her while she's still hot from cumming." Finally I was out of the way and Lou was fucking her, but her eyes never left me. Even when I moved around the room her eyes followed me. Lou busted his nut and a couple of the guys fucked her again or got blowjobs and then one of the guys said we had to break it up because his parents would be home soon. Everybody started dressing and leaving and I heard Patty say:

"Isn't anybody going to help me up?"

I went over to her and offered her a hand and pulled her up. She gave me a long steady look and then said thank you. I left and I didn't see her again for two years.

***

My parents moved to the same town where my aunt, uncle and cousin Lou lived. Because of an accident I had missed one semester of school and I had to attend one semester at the local high school and get my diploma before I could go on to college. The first day of school I was sitting in the cafeteria studying my class schedule when someone sat down across from me. I looked up to see a girl with flaming red hair and I knew right away that it was Patty.

"Remember me?" she said.

I smiled and said, "Of course I do."

She cocked her head to one side and said "Really," not as a question, but in surprise.

I said, "Really. There haven't been that many redheads in my life who have left claw marks on my body."

Patty actually blushed and then she said, "Lou told me that you moved here and I'd like to talk to you, but I need to get to my next class.

Can you meet me in the library at 3:30?"

I didn't have anything planned and I was curious so I said I'd be there. She was waiting for me when I got to the library and as I sat down I said:

"Okay, what do you want to talk about?"

I could see that she was trying to get up her courage up so I gave her a friendly smile and looked like I was eagerly waiting whatever it was she was going to say. Finally she said:

"Lou said you are only going to be here for one semester and then you are going to leave for college." I nodded a yes and she said, "Since you won't be here all that long I want to ask you for a favor. Can I be your steady girl while you are here?"

She caught me completely by surprise with that and I said, "Why in the world would you ask me that? You don't even know me."

She looked me right in the eye and said, "I know one thing about you. You are the only one who has ever made me cum."

I shook my head. "Patty, the circumstances had more to do with that than my sexual prowess. It was just will power on my part. You felt so hot that I didn't ever want to stop. And you were hot and wet because six other guys had done you before I got to you. To the best of my knowledge I haven't made any other girls cum."

She looked down at the table and said in a low voice, "You don't want anything to do with me because I've been everybody's whore."

Well, she was kind of right about that. She was a great looking girl, but if I dated her I'd be the butt of all the jokes from all the guys who had fucked her. She looked so downcast sitting across from me that I said:

"Tell you what. I have to study tonight, but I don't have anything on for tomorrow so why don't we get together and see what happens."

What happened was incredible. We went for a movie and then we went out to a secluded spot on the lake and spread a blanket on the ground. She gave me a blowjob that curled my toes, swallowed my cum (a first for me), kept her mouth on me until I was hard again and then we fucked, and we fucked, and we fucked some more. Every time I thought that it would be impossible for me to get it up again Patty proved me wrong. She had at least five orgasms and left claw marks all over my shoulders, back and ass cheeks. When she finally let me rest she smiled and said:

"I knew it. I just knew it. I knew it was you who made me cum and not just the circumstances of our first time."

I could hardly argue with her; she was only the sixth girl I'd made it with (not counting our first meeting) and not one of them had ever orgasmed or come even close to being as intense and as satisfying as Patty. She had my cock in her hand and was trying to stroke it back to life and when it gave a twitch she said, "Oh goody" and she went down on me. After a minute or so she stopped sucking and looked up at me:

"So, can I be your steady until you leave for college?"

I was going to argue with a girl who had my cock in her mouth?

***

During that school term I was the most hated guy in school, at least by the other guys. When Patty said she was my steady girlfriend she meant it and she cut off all the other guys who were used to fucking her whenever they wanted to. Patty was determined to drain everything she could out of me before I left for college and we fucked damn near every night. My studies suffered, but I still managed to keep passing grades. I actually started thinking that maybe I could flunk one or two classes just so I wouldn't have to leave Patty, but reason prevailed and I made up my mind that I would just have to go from the best fucked high school student in the state to whatever I could scare up in college.

While I was with Patty I learned a couple of things. She taught me how to eat her pussy and I grew to like doing it. She also had me fuck her in her ass, which was another first for me, and she told me how she had become the school's gangbang slut. Her mother worked afternoons and she was always left at home with her stepfather. One afternoon he had fucked her and after that he had fucked her two and sometimes three times a day whenever her mother wasn't home. Because of the fact that he gave her an orgasm almost every time he fucked her, she grew to love their encounters and she was devastated when he died in an auto accident. She was good-looking and boys started asking her out and when they tried to get into her pants she remembered how good it felt when her stepfather fucked her so she let them. But none of them ever came close to getting her off. One day a boy took her to a kegger and she got a little blitzed and ended up getting fucked by her date and about five of his friends. She almost had an orgasm, but by the time it was almost there the boys had gotten all of her that they wanted and they left her. She figured it would take quantity to get her where she wanted to go and the next thing she knew she was the school's gangbang girl. But she never again came even close to having an orgasm until the day that Lou brought me to her.

At the end of the fall semester I had all the credits that I needed for my diploma and I began getting ready to begin the winter term at college. Patty was trying hard to convince me that I didn't need college, that I could get a job and the two of us could stay together. But even as pussy whipped as she had me I was still smart enough to know that there wouldn't be much of a future for me with her and only a high school diploma. We made plans for a final weekend together and I stood her up because I didn't want to go through a final tear filled goodbye. I wasn't real proud of myself for doing it that way, but I was afraid she might be able to talk me into staying.

Where my last semester of high school had been pussy heaven, my first two years of college were a dry well. I dated several girls, but never found one that I liked all that much. I got laid a total of three times and all three were at parties where it got suddenly drunk out and things got a little out of hand. I'd gone six months without a sniff and I was bemoaning my fate to my roommate when he said:

"You have explained your problem to the right man, my son, and I, in my infinite wisdom, have seen the way to get you laid. Brush your teeth, comb your hair and I will lead you to the Promised Land."

It turns out that a good friend of his had hooked up with a freshman who loved to fuck and was willing to pull a train as long as the guys were clean and well behaved. We got to his friend's place and he introduced me and his friend said:

"She's already upstairs and going at it. You can go on up or have a beer or two and socialize. If you go up now there will probably be a line. If it was me I'd give the crowd a chance to clear out."

Good advice for some, but I remembered my first gangbang and how I felt when I slid into Patty's hot, wet, well fucked pussy and I wanted to feel it again and I didn't want to wait. I climbed the stairs and went to the designated room and had a bout of deja vu. On a mattress on the floor was a redhead with her skirt up around her waist and her legs up on the shoulders of the guy fucking her and there were five guys standing around waiting their turn. I had to blink my eyes because I thought I was seeing things, but I wasn't - it was Patty! She had her eyes closed, same as the first time and I moved off to the side so I could watch and it was like I had climbed into a time machine and gone back four years. Her eyes stayed closed during the next two guys and then suddenly they opened and she was looking right at me. I didn't see any change of facial expression, but from the moment she opened her eyes they never left me as guy after guy climbed between her legs and fucked her. I watched as she was double penetrated and triple penetrated and she never took her eyes off me, not once.

Finally we were alone in the room and she watched with an unreadable gaze as I undressed. As I moved between her spread legs she looked up at me and said:

"Make me cum, baby, please make me cum, it's been so long."

She was hot, she was wet, sloppy and loose and she felt absolutely marvelous. Patty clung to me and kept saying over and over again:

"Please, baby, I need it, make me cum, baby, make me cum."

Patty was so loose that I barely felt the walls of her pussy and because of the lack of friction I was able to fuck her for what seemed like hours. I felt her nails dig into me and she started moaning "Yesyesyesyesyes" and then a really loud "Oh god yes" and her body trembled and shook as she had an orgasm. She had two more before I finally had mine and when it was over she looked up at me and said:

"Take me out of here."

I dressed as she used her panties to clean up the cum that was all over her legs and crotch and then we left the party. I took her to my place and we fucked several more times. I don't know what it is that I have that makes Patty cum; whatever it was, it sure didn't work with the rest of the girls I'd been with. Sometime during the night Patty got up to go to the bathroom and when after a while she hadn't come back I got up to see if she was okay. I found her on the living room couch being fucked by my roommate. He had been on his way to the bathroom when she came out and he had taken her by the arm and had led her to the couch. I watched for a few minutes and then I went back to bed. Ten minutes later Patty came back into the room and began to suck my cock. When she had it up she climbed over me and lowered herself down.

"I know you like the feel of me when I'm full of cum so I let him fuck me. Stay with me, baby; don't run away from me again. You're the only one who can make me cum. I'll fuck as many guys as you want me to so I'll always be full of cum for you, just don't leave me again, baby. Please don't walk out on me again."

Patty moved in with me and my roommate and for the next two years we shared her, along with a few of our friends, because she was right - I did like, no make that love, the feel of her when she had someone else's juices in her. When I graduated with my degree in Electrical Engineering I kissed her goodbye. I would have taken her with me, but she was determined to stay and get her degree. We talked on the phone a lot and she seemed to get a big kick out of calling me while she was in the middle of a gangbang and letting me hear all the sounds. Just before she would hang up she would say:

"Hope you have a hard cock, baby. I miss you."

***

A year went by and though I dated a lot I was never able to find the sexual satisfaction that I found with Patty, but I was getting laid a lot and I guess that counted for something. And then suddenly the calls from Patty stopped and when I called her I kept getting the "This number is no longer in service" message. A couple of months went by and one night when I got home from work I found Patty sitting in the hallway outside my apartment. As I came down the hall toward her she stood up and said:

"Hey, mister, any chance a girl can get laid in this place?"

I took her in my arms and kissed her and said, "I wouldn't be the least bit surprised."

We were married three months later and my cousin Lou was my best man. As we drove away on our honeymoon Patty slid over next to me and took one of my hands and put it on her pussy. "Feel how wet I am? I know how much you like fucking me when I have someone else's cum in me so I fucked a few of your friends at the reception. Actually, I fucked Lou just before I walked down the aisle. You don't mind, do you?"

I pulled over to the side of the road and fucked her on the back seat.

We have been married almost fifteen years now and once or twice a week Patty will bring me a cum filled pussy and as I'm fucking her she will look up at me and say those familiar words:

"Make me cum, baby, make me cum."

End of the 5th Story

Herb, Tricia and Me

There are some that say that revenge is a waste of valuable time; time that could be put to more productive use doing other things. To me and to my way of thinking, good mental health requires payback when you are fucked over. You have a choice: In ten or fifteen years you can look back and say, "Damn it! I should have......" or you can look back and smile at what you did.

***

Tricia and I had dated and gone steady for a year and a half in high school and near the end of our junior year she dumped me for our team's starting quarterback. He - Danny - wasn't too bright or he never would have gotten together with her. I think he started to get the message the Friday night we played the Ypsilanti Braves and the right guard stepped aside and let his man through. The right guard (moi) did it three more times before I was pulled from the game and benched. By then Danny's bell had been rung once too often and he was pulled because he couldn't seem to get it together after that. Marty, the second stringer, went on in Danny's place, had one hell of a game and we beat Ypsi 24-21, but my football career was over.

The coach ripped me a new asshole for what I had done and threw me off the team, but not before asking me why. I told him straight up why I had done it and that I'd do it again if I had the chance. He called Danny in and asked him if it were true that he'd stolen my girlfriend and Danny puffed up his chest and cracked wise:

"It ain't my fault if he can't hang on to his women."

The coach just looked at Danny and then he shook his head and then said:

"Son, that's a team out there. You have to play together to win and to do that you need to be tight with your teammates. You just don't fuck over your teammates."

And he threw Danny off the team also. It ended up costing us both a chance at a football scholarship. It didn't hurt me because my parents could afford to send me to college, but Danny's couldn't. Danny was so pissed at being thrown off the team that he told Tricia to go to hell. She came crawling back to me and I told her to fuck off and die. Danny was popular and getting him thrown off the team pissed a lot of people off and Tricia (who got the blame instead of me) did not have a happy rest of her Junior year and she did not have all that good a time as a Senior either. She was the only girl in the senior class that didn't get asked to the prom.

There was one more unpleasant outcome from the mess. I tried out for football at Eastern Michigan as a walk on, but the coach didn't even give me a look. He told me he knew all about what I'd done and that no one with an attitude like that was ever going to play for him.

In a way it was probably a good thing since without football to get in the way I was able to knuckle down and graduate with a 3.91 GPA and that made me attractive to the XYZ Corporation and I went to work for them one week after being handed my sheepskin.

***

I didn't see Tricia after I left high school. Where I'd gone to Eastern Michigan, she had gone to the University of Michigan. My second day at XYZ I was sitting in the cafeteria looking over the choices I had to make on the insurance package when someone sat down across from me and set their tray on the table. I looked up from my paperwork and saw Tricia. She looked me right in the eye and said:

"Are you going to say hi?"

I looked at her for several seconds, said "Hi" and then went back to looking over my insurance benefits paperwork.

"Still holding a grudge?"

"I said hi. That's what you asked for and I gave it to you. Now, if you don't mind, I need to make my choices and turn the paperwork in."

"Okay, let's try it this way. I asked for a hi and you gave me what I asked for. While you are in a giving mood I'm going to ask you to forgive a stupid teenager for being a stupid teenager. Rob, we all did things that we regret doing when we were in junior high and high school. I screwed up. I'm sorry. Can't we at least be friends?"

I looked at her sitting across from me, still the best looking girl that ever went out with me and I figured, "What the hell, it can't hurt to be just friends" so I said:

"Okay. We can be friends."

She smiled and stuck out her hand and said, "Shake?" I took it and shook it and eleven months later I took her hand again and slid a ring on her finger as I said, "I do."

***

The next five years went by fast. Tricia and I decided that we wanted to wait for a while before having kids. We had places we wanted to go and things we wanted to do and we wanted to be a little more stable financially before starting a family. We sank all of our energy into each other and our jobs. We bought a three-bedroom house because we knew that one-day we were going to have children. We got passports and spent our vacations traveling and seeing the world.

By the end of that five-year period I began talking with Tricia about starting a family, but she told me she wasn't ready just yet. She had just been promoted to manager in her department and she had some things she wanted to do, some changes she wanted to make to make the department more efficient and to "leave her stamp" on it. I knew how she felt because I'd been made a section manager six months before and I'd had the same feelings.

I didn't really like her new job because she had to travel and would be gone for two or three days on the average of twice a month. But she loved her job and was happy so I decided not to push for kids until she hit 'the wall.' You do know about 'the wall' right? Every company that has been in business for a long time has a 'wall.' It is called the "Because that is the way we have always done it" wall. I knew that the entrenched bureaucracy would resist all the changes she wanted to make and eventually she would give up fighting them and at that point she would be ready to consider children. If my own experience at trying to make changes was any yardstick I only had about six months to wait.

***

Tricia had just left for a three day trip to Atlanta and I was sitting at my desk wondering what to do with my evenings while she was gone when my boss buzzed me and asked me to come into his office. He told me that there was a problem at our Charlotte facility and asked me to fly down and take a look. Naturally I said yes and he told me he would have his secretary make the arrangements. She called me at noon and told me she had me set up with a two-ten flight and that I would have to change planes in Atlanta. I told her about Tricia being in Atlanta and asked that since I had to change planes in Atlanta and wouldn't get in to Charlotte until too late to go into the office that she reschedule me. I'd overnight in Atlanta, spend the evening with Tricia and catch the first flight out to Charlotte in the morning. She called me back twenty minutes later and gave me the new arrangements.

I arrived in Atlanta and took the hotel courtesy bus to the hotel where Tricia was staying. I called her room from the lobby and got no answer so I asked the desk clerk for a key. After checking my driver's license information against Tricia's registration information she gave me a key card and I headed up to the room. It was my intention to surprise her when she came into the room, but I was the one who was surprised.

I entered the room and the first thing I thought was that I was in the wrong room. There were men's clothes hanging on the clothes bar and I was just about to back out of the room when I saw the monogrammed luggage I had given Tricia when she was promoted. I closed the door and looked around the room and found enough of Tricia's things to convince me that I was in her room all right. One look at the unmade bed with the wet spot in the middle told me the rest of the story. I took one last look around and then left.

I went down to the lobby and went into the gift shop and bought a copy of that day's Atlanta Constitution to hide behind and went out and sat down in the lobby where I could keep an eye on the front door and the elevators and settled in to wait. While I sat there waiting for Tricia to show I wondered at the lack of rage I was feeling. Why hadn't I waited in the room and then exploded on them when they came in. Why hadn't I sat there gleefully destroying everything that whoever the man was had left in the room? Why didn't I shred his clothes and cut up his suitcases? Why did I just look around and then leave? I honestly didn't know. I tried to think of what I might have done to drive Tricia to cheat on me, but I couldn't come up with a thing. She hadn't been any less loving or affectionate toward me. I had seen nothing that would have even remotely made me think she might be running around on me.

About an hour later I saw Tricia coming in the front door and I recognized the man with her. Herb Scott also worked at XYZ. He was a manager in the Marketing Department. The two of them walked hand in hand to the elevator and Herb pushed the call button. The two of them kissed while they waited for the elevator to come and then the door opened and they walked inside. When the door closed I got up from where I was sitting and went to the bank of payphones and called the airline and got myself on the last flight out of Atlanta for Charlotte. I might be leaving, but was I going to let her get away with it? Not on her life, but my revenge on the cheating whore was not going to be a screaming confrontation. I wanted much more satisfaction than that. I didn't yet know what I was going to do to them, but it was going to be something that the two of them would remember for the rest of their lives. I think it was the Italians who said:

"Revenge should be like a fine wine. It should be sipped and savored."

***

I landed in Charlotte and went to a bank of phones and called Tricia. When she answered the phone she sounded out of breath.

"Where were you, Rob? I called the house a couple of times and didn't get an answer."

"Not surprising since I'm downstairs in the lobby. I'll be right up."

"What!!"

"Yeah, lover. Charlie asked me to go to Charlotte and take care of a problem there. I had to change planes here in Atlanta and I thought I'd overnight here with you and go on to Charlotte in the morning."

"Here? You are here in the lobby?" I could hear the panic in her voice as she said, "Hold on a second, Rob; I left the water running in the bathtub and I need to turn it off."

I heard murmuring in the background and then a very distinct "Oh shit." I smiled at the image of her lover trying to get his shit picked up and out of the room. I could imagine him scurrying down the hall to the stairwell until I was in the room, or maybe dressing there and then going down the stairs to the front desk and trying to get a room while Tricia scrambled to make the bed and think of a way to explain the wet spot. I heard a door close and then Tricia came back on the line.

"Sorry to make you wait, love, but I didn't want the tub to

overflow."

"What was that "Oh shit" I heard?"

"In my hurry to get to the tub I stubbed my toe and it hurt."

"Oh, babe, I'm sorry."

"It wasn't your fault."

"Well, in a way it is. If I hadn't called to joke with you it wouldn't have happened."

"Joke with me?"

"Yeah, sweetie, I'm not in the lobby. I'm calling from Charlotte. I did have to change planes in Atlanta and I was going to surprise you, but I couldn't get a flight out in the morning early enough to get me here for my meeting so I couldn't stop over."

"Oh gee, honey, and you had me thinking I was going to get laid tonight instead of watching the dumb stuff on TV."

"Maybe I'll surprise you the next time. Hey, got to run. Here comes the hotel shuttle bus. I'll talk to you later, sweetie. Love you."

"I love you too, Rob. Bye."

I at least had the pleasure of knowing that I'd almost given Tricia and her asshole lover heart failure.

***

During my time in Charlotte and on the trip home, I thought about how I would take my revenge. I rolled a dozen plots and scenarios over in my mind and one by one I discarded them as either impractical or too hard to make happen. I got back to the main office and gave Charlie my report and as I was leaving his office I saw my revenge walking toward me. Marsha, Charlie's secretary, was just returning from the ladies room and she looked very uncomfortable waddling down the hallway. I wondered if Tricia would waddle like that and be as uncomfortable if she were eight months pregnant.

That night, Tricia's last night on her trip, I sat down and made a list of the things I needed to do to make it happen. None of it would be too difficult, but it would be time consuming which meant that I was going to have to pretend to be the loving husband. Frankly, I wasn't sure that I was a good enough actor to pull that one off, but I had to try.

First step in the plan would be to get Tricia pregnant even though she didn't want to be a mommy yet. Well no, that couldn't be the first step. The first step had to be getting Herb out of the picture. No, damn it, I couldn't do that either. I needed him for the confrontation if the plan was going to work. Okay, the first step had to be getting me ready and I knew just how to do that. Every summer the manager of our Dayton branch took three weeks vacation and every year Charlie asked for a volunteer to cover Dayton for the three weeks Ralph was gone. That year I was Charlie's volunteer.

The three weeks in Dayton was just what I needed. It gave me time to settle my anger and rage, which made it easier for me to play the part of loving husband when I got home. I talked with Tricia every night and we did all the bullshit "I love you" and "I miss you" and "I wish you were here with me" garbage while all the time I was wondering if Herb was with her in our house and fucking her on our bed.

I came home ready to implement my plan. I observed, I calculated, I charted and I planned and waited for the stars to align themselves. It took almost four more months, four months of pretending to be a loving husband, before everything fell into place. Tricia had another trip to Atlanta and I kissed her goodbye the morning she left and as soon as she was gone I picked up the phone, called Marketing and asked for Herb Scott. I was told he was in Atlanta on business and wasn't expected back for three days.

The timing was perfect for me. I went to Charlie's office and told him I had a family emergency and was going to need a few days off and then I caught a flight to Atlanta. I lucked out and got the same desk clerk and she remembered me. After comparing my driver's license against Tricia's registration information she gave me a key card and I went on up to Tricia's room. I knocked several times and no one came to the door so I let myself in and found the same set-up I had found the last time - Herb's clothes hanging on the clothes bar next to Tricia's clothes. That was all I really wanted to make sure of so I went on down to the lobby and waited.

I hid behind a paper and sat there until the two of them came in and got on the elevator and then I got up and went to the restaurant across the street and had my dinner. The time it took me to eat was about the amount of time I figured that it would take the two of them to get naked and be in the middle of things. I went back to the hotel, took the elevator to the fifth floor and took out my cell phone. I called the hotel's number and asked for Tricia's room. Just like that last time she sounded out of breath when she picked up.

"Oh hi, honey. I was just about to call you."

"You wouldn't have gotten me."

"No? Why not?"

"Remember the time I called you and jokingly told you I was in the lobby?"

"Yes, I remember."

"Well, sweetie, this time it is no joke. I'll be right up," and I disconnected.

It wasn't very sporting of me, in fact it was like shooting fish in a barrel. I was standing in front of room 507 when the door opened and

Herb came hurrying out. He had a suitcase in each hand and all he had on was a pair of boxers. He never saw it coming as I sent my right fist into his face with all of my hundred eighty-five pounds behind it. I felt his nose break and I saw blood shoot all over the place. He hit the floor at the feet of Tricia who had been hurrying along behind him carrying his clothes. She had pulled on a robe, but hadn't tied it and it was hanging open and I saw her naked body and I saw traces of wet cum on her inner thighs. She was looking at me with an expression of horror on her face.

"Some things never change, do they Tricia? First Danny and now Herb."

I gave Herb two hard shots in his nuts with the toe of my shoe and then I turned and walked away. I headed for the airport and caught the last flight home. I knew Tricia well enough to know that she wasn't going to rush home from Atlanta. She would stay there and do her job so I had two more days before I would see her again and I used those two days to get ready for the next step in getting back at Herb. As far as getting even with Tricia, I wasn't yet sure how that would go down. It would depend on what she did. If she came home begging for forgiveness and really wanted it, things would go the way I wanted. If not, what I had planned would still work, but wouldn't be near as satisfying.

***

Taking care of Herb was expensive, but if you want quality revenge you can't get it on the cheap. I knew a guy, who knew a guy, who had a friend, who knew a guy, etc., etc., and I managed to buy two pounds of marijuana and three ounces of cocaine. A Snap On tool salesman sold me a 'slim jim' and I was ready.

Like most XYZ traveling employees, Herb left his car in the company parking lot and took the company shuttle bus to the airport. I waited until after the building had cleared out and it was dark outside and then I slipped into Herb's office and planted half a pound of grass and an ounce of coke in the back of his lower left desk drawer. Next, I used the slim jim to pop his car's door lock and I put the rest of the grass and coke under the passenger side front seat. I locked the car back up and then I went home and waited. Over the next two days I kept an eye on Herb's car and the day I saw it gone I went down the street to a pay phone and called the police. I gave them Herb's name, address and car information and told them I had seen him selling dope to the employees at XYZ and then I hung up.

Two days later the employee cafeteria at XYZ was all-abuzz with:

"Did you hear what happened to Herb over in Marketing? He was arrested for dealing drugs."

"Darla over in Marketing said the police came to Herb's office with a search warrant and found drugs in his desk."

"Joe told me Herb got stopped for some traffic violation and they found drugs in his car."

"Fran said she heard that he pulled a gun on the cops and made a run for it."

"I was always suspicious of that weasel. I could tell he was no good just by looking at him."

Somehow Herb made bail and came into work only to be suspended pending an investigation into allegations that he was selling illegal substances on company property.

***

Meanwhile, Tricia had been calling me a half dozen times a day and I didn't take any of her calls. The day she returned she came into my office and closed the door behind her.

"May I sit down?"

I shrugged so she sat down on the chair on the other side of my desk. "You haven't been taking my calls."

"Given the circumstances under which I last saw you, that comes as a surprise?"

"I would have thought that you would have wanted to talk."

"What's to talk about? You replaced me."

"That's why we need to talk, Rob. I haven't replaced you. I could never replace you. I love you, Rob. I know you are upset over what you saw, but Herb means nothing to me. I need you to give me a chance to explain. Can we please sit down at home tonight and talk."

"Why? You going to try and make me believe that it never happened? That it was just some big hallucination and I really didn't see what I thought I saw?"

"No, Rob, I am going to try and convince you that I love you and that even though it did happen we can get by it."

"Not very likely, Tricia, but I'll give you a chance to talk. Now if you don't mind I'm very busy right now so please leave."

As she got up to leave I was smiling inside. It was going to work out the way I wanted it to.

***

Tricia had dinner ready and a bottle of wine sitting on the counter, uncorked and 'breathing'. This was Tricia's party and I kept quiet and made her work for it.

"First, Rob, you have to know that I love you. I have always loved you and no one is ever going to take your place in my heart. I want you, Rob; I don't want anyone else and you have to believe that. Herb was a mistake, a bad mistake and I should have known better after that first time."

"Why do you say that? Why didn't you know better before the first time?"

"Because I wasn't in any shape to know anything the first time."

"Can you explain that so a poor simple minded soul like me can understand?"

"The first time happened when I was drunk out of my mind. It happened on one of my office visits to Dallas. After the meetings the office staff and I went out for dinner and drinks. After dinner we went into the hotel lounge and had more drinks. You know how booze affects me, Rob, and you know I usually watch my drinking except when we are here at home. But I was in a hotel with a room right upstairs and I didn't have to drive home so I let myself go and enjoyed myself. By the time the people from the office left I was well on my way to being blitzed.

"I intended going up to my room when the last of our group left, but that is when Herb came in and saw me. He was in town on business and staying at the same hotel. He sat down with me, bought me a drink and we sat and talked and he bought me another drink and then another and the next thing I knew I was on my back naked and he was doing me. I had no recollection of leaving the lounge, undressing or being undressed, just all of a sudden I'm looking up at Herb. Given what he was just arrested for, for all I know he slipped something in one of my drinks and drugged me.

"You know me, Rob, and you know how I am when it comes to sex. Drunk or sober I get into it and even though I didn't know how Herb got there my body responded to what he was doing. He did me two more times and when he finished I fell asleep. In the morning when I woke up he was doing me again and when he finished he wanted me to call in and tell them I'd be late so we could do it some more and I told him to leave.

"That night I skipped dinner and went to my room. Around nine I got hungry and called room service. When there was a knock on my door I opened it expecting it to be room service, but it was Herb. He pushed by me into the room and started undressing and as I watched I thought, "Why not?" The damage had already been done and I was curious to see what he would be like when I was sober. That was the start of it."

"When did it start?"

"When I got promoted and started traveling. It was on my third trip."

"You have been fucking Herb for a year?"

"Yes and no. It has been a year, but it has only been five or six times. Just when we find ourselves visiting an office at the same time."

"So the other night wasn't planned in advance?"

"No, Rob, never. And I didn't go looking for him when I was on a trip, but if he came to me I never said no. That last trip he was at the airport when I got there and he talked the gate agent into seating us together. I don't have any good reason for it, Rob, it was just something to do when I was away from home. Something a little better than just sitting in my room watching TV."

"How many times did you fuck him in our house and on our bed while I was in Dayton?"

"I never saw him except for on trips. I swear to God, Rob, he was never in this house and I never did it with him except when we met on trips. If it hadn't have been for that first time it never would have happened, Rob. I guess I looked at it like, "We already have, the damage is done, and Rob will never know." I don't care a bit for Herb, honey. He never meant a thing to me."

"So that makes it okay? He didn't mean anything to you?"

"No, Rob, that doesn't make it okay. I fucked up and I'm sitting here asking you to forgive me. I'm asking you to believe that I love you and don't want to be with anyone but you."

"That's a tall order, Tricia, and I don't know that I'm the kind of man who can do it. What you did hurt me, Tricia. It hurt me bad and right now I want to hurt you. I want to strike out and make you pay for what you did to me. What makes it worse is that it is the same thing you did to me with Danny. I have something inside me screaming for revenge and I can't see any way on God's green Earth that I can forgive you while I feel that way."

"What can I do, Rob? I'll do whatever you want to prove to you that I love you and want to be with you. You want to beat me? Go ahead and do it and I'll clench my teeth and take it. Go ahead, Rob, take a belt to me; I'll stand still for it. I'm not kidding, Rob. I WILL do whatever you want as long as we stay together."

"What if what I want is to destroy that beautiful face of yours so that no man will ever want to look at you again? What if what I want is to carve the letter "A" for adulteress on your forehead or cheek?"

She looked at me for several seconds and then she said, "If that is what it will take to keep us together, I will accept it."

The thing of it was that I really believe she meant it. That was the first time since the whole thing started that I gave any consideration to the fact that she might actually love me. Not that it mattered. Her love for me might have been strong, but my love for her was gone. I stood up and she asked:

"Where are you going?"

"I can't stay in this house with you, Tricia, not the way I'm feeling right now. I'll need some time to think about what I'm going to do."

"Please, Rob, I'll do whatever I have to do, I swear I will."

"I'll think on it, Tricia, and get back to you in a few days or maybe a week or so."

She had a defeated look about her as I headed out of the house and God, but did I ever feel good about it.

***

I let her stew about it for five days and then I called her.

"I've decided what I'm going to do. The only way I will ever be able to live with you after what you did is if I do something to get back at you. You will have one chance and one chance only. If you do it we can start trying to put things back together. If you don't do it, I'll get an attorney and start divorce proceedings."

"What is it?"

"All you need to know is that tomorrow I will be at the house at five-thirty and you will meet me at the door naked and you will do everything I tell you to do without complaint. Just one "Oh no, I can't do that" or an "I won't do that" and I'm gone. I'll see you at five-thirty," and I hung up on her.

The next day I was there at five-thirty on the dot and she was waiting for me as I had specified. I handed her a bag and told her to take it into the bedroom and empty the contents on the bed. She did it and found three dozen condoms, a tube of KY Jelly and a sleep mask.

"What's all this?" she asked.

"It has to do with your punishment. When you told me your story of how you and Herb started, you said of the second night, "I was curious what he would be like if I were sober." That told me everything, Tricia. It told me that you wanted another cock. You were curious about another cock that wasn't mine and you used what had happened the night before between you and Herb as your excuse. So tonight we are going to satisfy your curiosity about other cocks. You are going to wear the sleep mask with a towel over it so that you can't see a thing and six men are going to fuck you. Six men that you know. Six men that you see at social gatherings. Six men, some of them the husbands and boyfriends of women you know and you will be blindfolded so you won't know who they are.

"They have been told what you did and that you are a cheating whore and they are going to use you any way they want until they don't want you anymore. They are going to use your mouth, your unfaithful cunt and your ass and some of them might even want to use all three at once. That is your punishment, Tricia; that is how I will get even with you. Every wedding, every funeral, every cocktail party, birthday party, Christmas party or dinner party you go to you will see men and you will look at them and wonder if any one of them was one of the men who fucked you and knew you for the filthy whore you are. Every woman you face will have you wondering, "Did I fuck your husband and if you knew, would you still talk to me or would you spit in my face?

"Some of the men who will fuck you have a close enough relationship with their wives or girlfriends that they can tell them what happened here tonight and why. Everyone has promised absolute secrecy on this so none of them will ever let you know who they are. You will see women and wonder, "Does this woman know that I'm a whore who cheated on my husband and then gangbanged six men? Does that woman know that her husband degraded me by fucking me in my ass or had me stand in the bathtub while he pissed on me?

"I have no idea what the six will do to you, Tricia, and I don't care. They may settle for just pissing in your mouth or they may only want to gangbang your ass repeatedly, but whatever they do or want to do, you will let them. One refusal on your part, however minor, and I walk away. The condoms are for their use if they want your cunt, but your ass and mouth get raw cock."

I looked at my watch. "They will be here any minute now. Your choice, Tricia: either put the sleep mask on or put a robe on and cover yourself."

She stared at me in silence and I thought I saw a tear in the corner of her right eye, but then she picked up the sleep mask and put it on.

By three in the morning it was over. The six didn't want anymore and Tricia was a fucked out mess. She had cum all over her body and her cunt and asshole were gaping canyons. The six had treated her like a worthless whore and had called her every derogatory name in the book as they used her. Her nipples had been pinched and twisted hard, her ass had been slapped and cocks had been pushed into her mouth so hard she had gagged and choked. When the last of the six had gone, I told Tricia to take off the towel and sleep mask.

"I'm going back to the motel and check out. I want you and this room spotless when I get back and then we will see to the second part of your punishment."

"Second part? What second part?"

I held her birth control pills in front of her and said, "You won't be using them anymore. Get ready to be a mommy."

"But my job? If I get pregnant I won't be able to keep working after I have the baby."

"Other women find a way. Besides, if you are not working, you won't be traveling and I won't have to wonder about what you are doing in your hotel room and with whom. Anyway, it is not debatable. We do it my way or I'm out of here. Are we clear on that?"

There was a moment of silence and then she said, "Yes, Rob."

***

It took me an hour to go to the motel and check out. When I got back to the house Tricia was showered and had changed the sheets on the bed and had straightened the bedroom. I made a big show of flushing her birth control pills down the toilet and then I crawled in bed with her and fucked her twice before falling asleep.

Even though her cunt was loose and I barely felt the sides, it was still a very satisfying fuck session in that I knew I had taken my revenge. How, you ask? Timing, it was all in the timing. I needed Tricia to go on a trip, be with Herb and then come back at a certain time. And then I had to schedule things just right. Tricia made her trip, I did my "catch her in the act" routine and then went home and waited for her to return. I let her tell her story and then I stalled talking to her for the five days I needed to get just the right night for my revenge. If all my calculating and planning was correct the night of Tricia's gangbang was the most fertile night of her cycle.

When the six men fucked her, I made a big production out of having her roll the condoms on the men before they fucked her, but what she didn't see because of the blindfold was each man cut the end off the rubber before he fucked her and when the night was over she never saw the modified rubbers because they were flushed as soon as the man finished. I'm sure she figured out that one or two might have broken; why else would she be so sloppy, but not to worry because she was on the pill, right? Wrong!!! I had been doctoring her pills for the last two months and she wasn't protected at all. I wasn't worried about me getting her pregnant because on my three-week trip to Dayton I'd gotten a vasectomy. Any kid conceived before the gangbang would be Herb's and after the gangbang it could be anybody's.

I made a big show of putting our marriage back together. I told Tricia that Herb and the night of revenge would never be mentioned again; that we were even and could get on with our lives. It was hard to pretend to be a husband trying to put what his wife had done behind him, forgive her and work to repair the marriage when it was the last thing on my mind. Tricia was history the day I found out about Herb and the only reason I was with her was for revenge. I'd never forgotten what she did to me with Danny. I had forgiven her for it, but I had never forgotten it. When Herb happened Danny came back to the surface and to paraphrase an old saying:

"Fuck over me once and shame on you. Fuck over me twice and shame on me."

There would not be a third time.

About a month after the gangbang Tricia told me I was going to be a daddy. I of course knew that it wasn't mine and given the timing it couldn't have been Herb's so the father had to be one of the six from the gangbang, which was the plan all along. I played loving husband and happy prospective father until it was too late for Tricia to abort and then I packed my bags and moved out. I told Tricia that I was sorry, but I just could not get past her cheating on me with Herb.

I got an apartment and then I sued for divorce on the grounds of infidelity and asked for the house, the cars, the checking and savings and half of her 401k and pension. Tricia got a lawyer and in our first conference her lawyer claimed I had no proof of Tricia committing adultery. I had no private investigator reports, no film or tape and no audio. It was a case of her word against mine and she was denying it and she was counter suing and she wanted the house, the cars, the checking and savings and half of my 401k and pension plus alimony and substantial child support.

I laughed and said I had all the proof of her infidelity that I needed in the baby she was carrying. I demanded and got a DNA test and it showed that little Sarah Anne wasn't mine. After that things moved along rather quickly. I got favorable rulings from the judge on a couple of things - he made Tricia pay my attorney's fees and all court costs, and I didn't have to pay alimony or child support, but everything else was split 50/50. We were each given the car we drove, but the house had to be sold and the proceeds split between us.

I saw Tricia in the courtroom the day the divorce was granted. She was crying when she said to me, "How could you do this to me, Rob? I loved you."

"But not enough to stay away from Herb. If you had come to me after that first time and told me what happened we would have been okay. I could have gotten by one drugged or drunken indiscretion, but not a year's worth. Goodbye, Tricia."

It was not the last time I saw her. We both still work for XYZ and I see her maybe three times a week and when I do, I ignore her.

***

There was one other part of my revenge and that was what I had done to Herb. He was offered a plea bargain and he, knowing full well he was innocent, turned it down and went to trial. The jury didn't believe his story that he was framed and he was found guilty and sentenced to prison. Two years into his sentence I visited him. As I sat on the other side of the glass partition with the phone in my hand I could see the curious expression on his face. I smiled at him and said:

"Wondering why I'm here, Herb? Simple. I just want the answer to a question. Have you been having a good time in here, Herb? Was fucking my wife worth it?"

I smiled at him as the realization dawned on him and I hung up the phone and got up and left.

End of the 6th Story

Jumping to Conclusions

I left the apartment at my usual time and pulled out of the parking lot onto the street. I turned and headed down Cortez to the stop sign at Monte Vista and then hung a left. Twenty minutes would have me at work and if it was a normal Friday and the day had no surprises I would be able to leave work early and head for the lake. I had the tent and the rest of the gear in the back of the pickup and all I would need to do is stop and get ice.

I reached over and turned on the radio and caught the last of George Jones doing 'The Cold Hard Truth.' The song ended and the DJ said:

"Nobody does it like 'Ole Possum' and now here is Susan with traffic and weather."

Susan told me that there were no tie-ups on my route and that my weekend would be warm and sunny. After a half dozen commercials for services I would never use and products I would never buy the DJ came back:

"Good morning. It is 7:06 on this beautiful Friday the ninth of June and you are listening to KXYZ. Here is Rhonda Vincent to take you for a ride on 'The Bluegrass Express.'"

I love Rhonda Vincent and The Rage, but I reached over and turned the radio off. The ninth of June. I'd totally forgotten that the day was the ninth of June. How the hell could I have forgotten that? The ninth of June. The day my marriage ended. It had taken some time to try and put that day behind me, but the memory was always there and as I drove to work it all came back to me.

***

It started with a business trip to Chicago. I'd kissed my wife Shari goodbye, told her I'd call her as soon as I got to Chicago and checked into the hotel. The flight was uneventful and I took the courtesy bus to the hotel and then called Shari to let her know where she could reach me.

I sat at the table in the room and reviewed the papers I would be going over with the customer the next day and around seven I headed down to the hotel restaurant to get a bite to eat. After a fairly decent top sirloin I went into the hotel lounge to listen to the live band and have a drink or two.

I was sitting at the bar nursing a vodka tonic when a throaty voice behind me said into my ear:

"Want me to suck your cock, honey?"

I quickly turned and saw Annette Carlson standing there. Annette had been my steady girlfriend during my first two years of college. We had torn up our share of bed sheets during those two years and had parted somewhat amicably when she told me that she wanted to fuck other guys. Her exact words were still burned into my memory.

"I like you a lot, Frank, but I was a virgin when we met and I want to experience some life while I'm still young."

Until the moment she laid that on me I was actually considering getting a ring and going to a knee in front of her. The quickness with which I dropped that idea told me that it probably wouldn't have been all that great an idea in the first place. I heard later that she had developed a reputation as 'an easy piece' around campus. And here she was fifteen years later standing behind me in a hotel bar in Chicago.

She threw her arms around me, hugged me and told me that it was so good to see me and then she invited me to join her and her husband at their table. I told her no thanks, that I didn't want to intrude and she said:

"Nonsense. Come on," and she grabbed my arm, pulled me off my stool and led me over to where her husband sat waiting. On the way to their table she leaned close and said:

"You don't have to mention my greeting to you. Harry wouldn't understand."

"Too bad. I was giving some serious thought to taking you up on your offer."

That of course wasn't true. I had never cheated on Shari and I never intended to, but it seemed like the thing to say at the time. Annette introduced me to her husband and then we proceeded to bore the poor guy to tears as Annette and I went through the old friends ritual of "Have you heard from_____," "Whatever happened to_____" and "Did you hear about_____."

Harry got up to use the men's room and Annette watched him walk away. When he was out of sight she said:

"Why did you ever let me get away?"

"As I remember it I didn't let anything happen. You just flat out told me that you wanted to sample the male population at school and you said goodbye."

"Biggest mistake of my life. I already had the best and didn't know it."

"Thanks, I think."

"It's true, baby, and you know it. Besides being a super nice guy, you had the best cock that I've ever had in me and I was stupid to let you get away."

"That isn't a nice way to talk with your husband just down the hall."

"Harry is a sweetheart and I'm glad I have him, but he is only so-so in the bedroom. He is what I picked and I knew what I was getting when I got him, but that doesn't mean I have to flush memories down the toilet."

Harry came back and the conversation turned to things that included him and we sat there, talked and drank for about an hour. Then Annie's cell phone rang and after saying hello the conversation went:

"I suppose."

"I'll have to ask Harry."

"Hey! You remember Frank Corbett?"

"He's sitting across from me right now."

"Hang on; let me check."

She turned to me. "You remember Mary Ellen Frasier?" I nodded a yes. "She's Mary Ellen Watson now. She's having a party and there will probably be a few others there you know. Want to go?"

I had nothing better to do so I said yes. Then I said that I needed to run up to my room first and Annie asked me if she could come up and use my bathroom.

"I'd rather use a real towel to clean up with instead of the paper towels in the ladies' room here."

As we walked to the elevators Annie, who had taken on a few more drinks than I had, giggled and said:

"I hope that no one who knows me is seeing this."

"Seeing what?" her husband asked.

"Me going up to a hotel room with two men."

Her husband said, "It will probably look even worse than that. They will see your husband leaving you and letting you to go up to a room with a strange man. God knows what they would think about that."

"Why? Where are you going?"

"To get the car. I'll meet you out front."

He went off and Annie and I got on the elevator. As the door closed behind us Annie giggled again and said:

"It's a good thing I love my husband or I'd make good on my earlier offer right here in this elevator. Would you let me, baby? Would you let your old girlfriend suck your dick?"

Knowing that she was just being playful I said, "You bet your sweet ass I would."

Let me be honest here. Annie was one hell of a sexy looking woman and she had been superb when it came to sucking cock so even though I had no intention of doing anything, her looks and the memory of her magic mouth had given me a hard on and she noticed. She reached down and touched the bulge, stroked it and giggled as she said:

"It remembers me. Can I see it? For old times sake?" and she reached for my zipper.

I was just reaching down to push her hand away when we reached my floor and the elevator door opened. Annie snatched her hand away, but not before the couple waiting for the elevator saw it. The woman looked away embarrassed and the man gave me a knowing grin as we exited the elevator and Annie giggled and said "Oops."

We entered my room and Annie used the bathroom while I got my address book and a pen out of my briefcase. I wanted it so I could enter the addresses and phone numbers if there were a lot of people at Mary Ellen's that I knew. Annie came out of the bathroom and I went in and checked myself in the mirror and saw the 'five o'clock' shadow. I grabbed the electric razor and did a quick clean up, left the bathroom, got Annie and headed downstairs. Harry was waiting out front and we drove over to a house on Chicago's south side.

Besides Mary Ellen, I knew a good half dozen of the people there from my college days. It was a very enjoyable evening and as far as I was concerned it was over too soon. I told several that I wanted to stay in touch and I put their phone numbers and addresses in my book. Harry and Annie drove me back to the hotel and I went to bed.

***

The next day went well and I called Shari and told her I would be home by eight. In a husky voice she said:

"Then I'll expect you in our bedroom at eight-oh-one and you had better be ready for a hot welcome home."

Thoughts of the feast waiting for me had me hard as a steel bar when I walked into the house at seven fifty-six. I dropped my suitcase and briefcase on the living room floor and headed for our bedroom.

I walked through the door and saw Shari spread on the bed in garter belt, high heels and nylons just as I was grabbed by several pairs of hands. I was caught off guard and the four men had forced me down on a chair before I could even begin to struggle. When I did begin to yell and struggle, a pair of socks was stuffed into my mouth and then with rope that they already had handy they tied me to the chair.

Shari got off the bed and walked over to stand in front of me.

"Do I look good, baby? Do I look hot in your favorite garter belt and nylons? How about my heels? They are your favorite 'come fuck me' pumps. I wanted to look my best for you as I give you your very own private porn show."

She turned and walked to the bed where the four men, one of whom I recognized as a guy she worked with, now sat naked with hard ons. She went to her knees in front of the one on the left, looked over at me and winked, and then she went down on him. Until then I had been struggling in a vain attempt to get loose, but when her mouth closed on the man's cock all the fight went out of me and I died inside.

Shari worked her way along the line of sitting men always looking at me and smiling before she took the man in her mouth. She spent about two minutes on each man and then went back to where she started and ran the line again. Next she got on the bed and spread herself wide and took the four men on one after the other and when all four were finished they took a break and went into the kitchen for I'm guessing some refreshment, after which they came back.

Shari got on the bed and took them on two at a time. While one fucked her, she sucked on a second one while the other two played with her breasts and kissed her on the neck and ears. Then one took her ass while another fucked her in the cunt. I could see that her nipples were hard and the men playing with her tits moved to suck on them.

There was no slow and easy fucking. The men fucked her hard and she was very vocal in her appreciation. After they had all cum a second time, they adjourned for more refreshment. When they came back Shari took off the garter belt and the by now laddered and cum soaked nylons, but she slipped her heels back on. She looked over at me and said:

"Thank you for this. I'm having more fun than the law should allow and I owe it all to you. I don't know if you enjoyed that whore you had in your hotel room as much as I'm enjoying this, but thank you for giving me the opportunity."

She turned to go back to her herd and as I looked at her back as she walked away, I was confused. I gave her the opportunity? Then it hit me! "The whore in your room last night." Somehow she had learned about Annie and had totally misread things. I was being paid back for a wrong that I had never committed and Shari would never know it because after what she was now doing I doubted that I would ever speak to her again.

When she got back on the bed she said to her crew, "I want to try something that I've read about. Any of you guys heard of making a girl airtight?"

One of them smiled and said, "Dibs on your ass" and Shari laughed as the four men moved her into position. The guy who called 'dibs' on her ass laid down and Shari moved over him and eased his cock into her ass as she settled onto him in the reverse cowgirl position. Then she leaned back and another guy moved into her in the missionary position. The two men started working into her trying to establish a working rhythm. The guy under her supported her with his hands so her hands were free. The remaining two men took a position on either side of her and she looked at me and winked before she took the one on her right into her mouth and the one on her left into her hand and started stroking him. After that it was just bodies moving around as the four men used her and she moaned and screamed and had orgasms.

Then it was over and the four men dressed and left.

"Just a little longer, baby," she said as the last of them went out the door. "I need to clean up and then we will have a little talk."

She went into the bathroom and I heard the shower start. It was almost a half hour before she came back into the room still naked. She had combed her hair and put on fresh makeup and she walked to the closet and got a robe and put it on. She came over to me and took the socks out of my mouth and as she started to untie the ropes holding me to the chair she said:

"What you just saw, baby, is what I'll do every time you cheat on me. I'm almost – notice I said almost – hoping that you might cheat a lot. It was awesome. I could get used to it if I let myself."

The ropes fell away and I tried to stand, but hours of being tied so that I couldn't move had their effect on me and I staggered and almost fell and had to grab the chair to keep from falling to the floor. Shari said:

"Come over here and sit down on the bed and we will talk."

I ignored her and stumbled toward the bathroom, but didn't make it before I fell to the floor. Shari came over to help, but I snarled at her to get the fuck away from me. I took a long overdue piss, splashed some cold water on my face, dried off and then walking a little better, I left the bathroom and walked through the bedroom to the stairs and started down them. Shari was behind me.

"Where are you going? We have to talk, Frank. We have to get some things straight."

I ignored her and walked to where I had dropped my suitcase and briefcase when I'd gotten home, picked them up and walked out of the house. Shari was standing in the front doorway calling out:

"Where are you going, Frank? This isn't helping any. Get back here. We have to talk."

She was still yelling at me as I backed down the drive, turned right when I got to the street and drove off. I found a motel close to work, checked in, left a call for six in the morning, got into bed and fell into a troubled sleep.

***

When the call from the desk came I got up, showered and then headed to the Village Inn for breakfast. While eating I made a mental list of what I needed to do that morning. At eight I called my boss and let him know that I was back in town, but had some personal business I needed to take care of and that I'd be in around noon.

By nine I had cleaned out the bank accounts and taken everything of value out of the safe deposit box. I walked down the street to a different bank and opened new accounts and got a new safe deposit box. By ten I'd cancelled all of our credit cards except for my American Express and one Visa card that was in my name only.

I called Shari's office and asked for her and as soon as she said hello and I knew that she was at work, I hung up and drove home. By eleven I had everything I needed to get me through the next couple of weeks.

When I got to work the receptionist handed me a stack of message slips and two thirds of them were from Shari. I separated them from the pile and dropped them into the trash can sitting next to Carol's desk. Then I told Carol that Shari and I had separated and not to take any more messages from her or put any of her calls through to me.

I stopped in at Ben's office and brought him up to date on my meetings in Chicago and then told him I might have to take some unscheduled vacation time. I told him that Shari and I had separated and I needed some time to find an apartment and move in. He asked me if I could hold off on taking the time off for a couple of days.

"I need you to go to Atlanta and handle a situation there. You will probably be gone four or five days."

I told him "No problem" and it really wasn't. It would get me out of town and away from anything that Shari might try. I would almost bet that by the time I left Ben's office Shari would have been declined on her credit cards. She wouldn't be able to get me by phone so she would probably come to my office, but by then I should be in the air on my way to Atlanta.

I cautioned Ben and Carol against letting Shari know I had gone out of town and then I hit the motel, got my stuff and headed for the airport. As I waited for my flight to be called I grabbed one of those free apartment finders magazines and started going through it and making a list of places to check out when I got back to town.

About halfway to Atlanta it occurred to me that I had forgotten something important. I used the in flight phone to call Ben and tell him to take my paycheck off of 'direct deposit' and hold it for me until I could get back and change it to my new bank.

While I had him on the phone he told me that he had talked to Shari. When she couldn't get me on the phone she insisted that Carol put her through to Ben. She tried to badger Ben into making me take her calls and Ben had told her that I had told him we were separated and then he told her that communication between her and me were not a company problem and he was not going to get involved and then he had hung up on her.

***

When I got into Atlanta I checked into a hotel and got a good night's sleep. The next day was spent putting out fires at the Atlanta office and when I got back to the hotel, I called my parents, my brother George and my sister Mary and brought them up to speed on my separation from Shari. I didn't go into detail, I just told them I came home from a business trip early and found something that I didn't care for. My mom told me that Shari had called and asked mom to have me call her which of course I didn't.

The next morning at nine I called Ben to give him an update and he surprised me. After telling me that he had seen Shari the previous evening, "I guess since she couldn't get you on the phone she decided to wait in the parking lot for you to get off work" he said:

"How do you like Atlanta?"

"I've only been here a few times, but it seems like a nice place."

"Is your separation from Shari a temporary thing while you try to work some things out, or is it something that will end up in a divorce?"

"There is no chance of us getting back together."

"Then how would you feel about moving?"

"What do you mean?"

"This is the third time I've had to send somebody to Atlanta to fix things. I'm going to let Falstaff go. Would you like the Atlanta office?"

"Hell yes I would."

"Okay then, you have it. We will work out the details when you get back."

It was a hell of a boost to my ego and as I sat there smiling, it occurred to me that a move to Atlanta would take away the hassle of trying to avoid Shari and it would have been a hassle. If she was going to sit in parking lots and wait for me what else would she try? I wasn't afraid to face her; I just didn't want to.

From the way she had talked as she untied me it was obvious to me that her mindset was "Okay, now we are even and we can put this behind us" but there was no way that was ever going to happen. If she had gone out and screwed some guy in a motel room and then come home and told me "Okay, now we are even" our marriage would still have been over, but for her to do what she did with four men and expect me to accept it? No way! No fucking way!

All a face to face would accomplish was I would probably spit in her face. I knew why she had done it and I wasn't at all happy with that. She didn't trust me enough to give me the benefit of the doubt until she could talk with me? Fuck her! No sir, better to just walk away. I wasn't going to go for a divorce! I was just going to walk away.

***

I finished up in Atlanta and headed for home. I left the airport and checked into a hotel close to work and then I went in to the office and brought Ben up to date. We talked about my taking the Atlanta office and set a timeline for it to happen. Then I took a couple of days off to take care of some personal business.

I was parked down the street from the house when Shari went to work and as soon as she turned the corner, I punched a number in on my cell phone, said we were good to go, and a couple of minutes later a Ryder rental truck driven by my brother George pulled onto the drive way. Behind it a car pulled in and parked and Skip and Cory, two very good friends of mine, got out and joined George and me. In two hours I had everything I wanted out of the house. I took all of my personal things, the home desktop computer, printer and enough furniture to set me up in an apartment in Atlanta.

I saw an attorney and had him draw up a power of attorney for my brother and then I put a copy of it in an envelope along with a note that said:

"Call George when you are ready to sell the house. He will act for me."

I didn't bother to sign it and I dropped it in the mail. She would get it in about two days and by then I would be on the road to Atlanta. I didn't care about the house. We had refinanced to put in the swimming pool and tennis court and I doubted that there would be any equity to speak of when the costs of selling were deducted from the proceeds.

I had one more stop to make and I told the man what I wanted, gave him some money and then I drove over to the place where I had rented the truck and they hooked a car hauling trailer on the back. I drove to George's house and loaded my car on the trailer and a half hour later I was Atlanta bound.

***

I called Ben and let him know that I was in place in Atlanta and he set his plan in motion. He flew into Atlanta that night and the next morning he went into the office and terminated Falstaff and sent all the people home for the day after telling them there would be no loss in pay and for them to return to work the next morning.

I'd spent the day checking out apartments and had settled on one by the time I met Ben for dinner. Over dinner he told me that Shari had been in the parking lot almost every day and sometimes twice a day – in the morning trying to catch me coming in to work and then again in the evening to catch me when I got off.

"Once she even stopped Carol and offered her a hundred dollars to get her past the security guard in the lobby and get her up to your office. It appears that she still doesn't know that you are gone."

The next morning we were in the office to greet the staff when they came to work. Ben brought them up to date on what was happening, wished me luck and then headed for the airport.

The next week and a half were spent moving into my new apartment, gathering the reins of my new office and getting to know my staff while they got to know me.

***

On the last Friday of the second week I received a package in the mail and I set it aside for review over the weekend. My apartment was on the second floor and had a small balcony that overlooked the swimming pool. I bought a small patio table and two chairs for use on the porch. Saturday morning I sat at the table drinking coffee and going through the contents of the package I'd received.

It had cost me a pretty penny, but I felt that it was well worth it. Operating on the assumption that Shari had enlisted Steve (he was the co-worker that I had recognized) to help her organize the gangbang and that they had set it up in a day I was sure that he used some of his buddies to fill out the gang. I gave the private detective all that I knew about Steve and then I gave him the physical descriptions of the other three men that had been there with him that night. I told the detective that I wanted him to follow Steve and see if Steve met with anyone who fit the descriptions and if so get me the information on them.

The results were way better than I expected. Steve had indeed met several times with three men who fit the descriptions that I had given the detective and a stroke of pure luck confirmed that the three were the men I wanted to find. The operative that had been following Steve saw him meet the three in a sports bar and he had gotten the booth next to them. He overheard them discussing the gangbang and talking about when they could do it again. He didn't hear if it was going to happen because he had gotten up to call for help in following the three when they left the bar. It had been hideously expensive, but I had the names, addresses, and places of employment of all four of the assholes. I began to make plans.

**

It was three months before I was able to arrange a weekend trip. I drove – no airline trail for anyone to follow – and I carried extra gas in cans so no fuel stops would trip me up. When I went into work on Monday morning, I was carrying the satisfaction of knowing that it would be a hell of a long time before Steve Bowen used his sexual equipment again. Cast iron pipe applied repeatedly to the crotch area sometimes had a detrimental effect on the male reproductive organs. It seems that a hooded man had caught Bowen in his apartment parking lot and stomped the shit out of him before taking his watch, rings, wallet and everything that was in his pockets.

Three weeks later the same thing happened to Archie Mellon and Jeff Montrose. By the time I made my third trip Norm Reed had apparently figured out what Bowen, Mellon and Montrose had in common and he took a job in another state and got the hell out of Dodge. Pity, but three out of four wasn't bad. I debated hiring a private detective to find him, but then decided not to.

The next five months went by and the job was going well. I'd met several of the bikini clad ladies that lounged around the apartment pool and I got to know a couple very well. One, a flight attendant named Brandy, managed to find her way into my bed and when she wasn't flying or visiting her folks she was keeping time with me. It was a good arrangement for both of us until the day she told me that she was getting married to one of the captains she regularly flew with. I guess when she wasn't in my bed she was in his when they overnighted somewhere. As a parting gift she did set me up with another flight attendant named Gloria and we hit it off. Gloria let me know up front that she wasn't interested in anything but a friends with benefits relationship which suited me just fine.

I was in the dumps for a couple of days after losing Brandy and before hooking up with Gloria and then it got worse. I got home from work one Tuesday night, pulled into the parking lot, shut off the car, got out and heard:

"Hello, Rob."

I turned and there stood Shari. I just stood there and stared at her.

"Surprised to see me?"

"More disappointed than surprised."

"Disappointed?"

"I hoped that I'd never set eyes on you again. The way I left you should have told you that."

"Maybe it would have if you had filed for divorce. The fact that you haven't made me hope that we could patch things up and get on with our life together."

"No chance of that. Your gangbang put an end to that."

"How can you hold that against me after what you did?"

"I don't even know what it is that I'm supposed to have done."

"Bullshit, Frank. I told you that I was getting even with you for having that whore in your room when I called."

"I didn't have a whore in my room, Shari."

"Don't give me that, Frank. I called you and a woman answered the phone. I asked her who she was and she told me and then asked who I was. When I said I was your wife she giggled and said:

"Oh, you are the lucky one who gets his great cock all the time" and then she hung up on me."

"So you, without bothering to talk to me about it, got stupid and had a gangbang to teach me a lesson. That about cover it?"

"Exactly!"

"First of all, Annie wasn't a whore. She and her husband were waiting for me to use the bathroom in my room and then they were going to take me to a party where there were some people I went to school with. Annie had taken on a few more drinks that she probably should have and she was probably trying to be cute when you called."

"Get off it, Frank. She flat out as good as told me that she was aware of your cock size."

"She was. Annie was my girlfriend through my first two years of college and then we broke up. Again, she was with her husband. All of that you could have found out if you had bothered to talk to me before ruining our marriage. As far as divorcing you is concerned it was in my best interest not to file, but let you do it."

"How do you figure that?"

"I would have had to split our assets equally with you if I had filed before I left."

"You will still have to even if I do file."

"Maybe, but the assets we would have to split would be the assets we held jointly at the time of filing and as of right now that is only the house and there isn't enough equity in it to waste time on."

"If you are going to wait on me to go for a divorce you've got a long wait coming. As long as we are married there is always a chance."

"No, Shari, there isn't a chance in hell. You showed me what you really think of me when you put on your display of pique. You showed me that you have no trust in me and you showed me that you thought I was a spineless wimp who would just accept what you did and say:

"Sorry. I'll be a good boy from now on."

"You killed the marriage, Shari, and there is no way in hell that it can ever be resurrected."

"You are wrong. I don't think you are spineless. I expected you to be outraged just as I was when that woman spoke to me on the phone. I know you aren't a wimp. That's why I had them tie you to the chair to keep you under control. I love you, Frank. I love you, want you and need you."

"That's just too fucking bad, Shari, because I don't want you. Not after being tied in that fucking chair and watching you for hours. You know what struck me the most as I sat there? The ease with which you did it and how quick you managed to set it up. As if it was something that you had done many times before. You seemed very comfortable with those four guys. It was almost like you were attuned to each other. Reliving a shared experience as it were."

Her face paled. "Oh no, oh no, Frank. Never. I swear to God, never before."

"Unfortunately, Shari, I don't have any trust in you anymore so I don't believe it. But no matter; the once was enough. Look on the bright side. You did say it was awesome and that you could get used to it so now you can. Call your four studs and have at it."

"I couldn't even if I wanted to."

"Why not? I'm certainly not going to be in the way."

"You know why not. You know what you did and even if they can't prove it, they know it was you."

"Sorry, Shari. I have no idea what you are talking about."

"I'm not stupid, Frank. When three of the four end up in the hospital emergency room and the only thing they have in common was that evening with me, it wasn't all that hard to figure out who was responsible."

"Only three? Why not four?"

"Because Norm figured it out too and moved out of town before you could get to him."

"Any idea where he went?"

"Why would you want to know?"

"Just curious."

"You aren't that good a liar, Frank."

"So those four aren't available, so what? You came up with those four quick enough. It shouldn't be all that hard for you to come up with some different guys."

"I don't want any other guys. I want you. I've put the house up for sale and as soon as it is sold I'm moving here to Atlanta."

"Why in the hell would you want to do that?"

"To be close to you. There isn't any way we can put things back together if we are six hundred miles apart."

"Haven't you heard anything I've said? We will not be getting back together. You being here and me seeing you from time to time will only remind me of you and your four fuck buddies and that is a memory that I am trying to get rid of, not reinforce."

"Say what you will, Frank, but I intend to get you back. It might not be easy and it might take a while, but I am going to do it."

"In a pig's ass," I said as I turned from her and went into my apartment. I never did ask her how she'd found me. Hired a private detective I suppose. I did wonder why I hadn't heard the phone ring when she called. It must have been when I was using my electric razor.

***

She did sell the house and move to Atlanta and she managed to get an apartment in the same apartment complex where I lived. Not in the same building thank God, but still way too close to suit me. It seemed like every night when I came home from work there was a note slipped under my door telling me that she was making one of my favorites and inviting me over for dinner. Notes inviting me to go to this or that with her or to meet her after work for a drink. I ignored all of them, but the one I found last night had me thinking. It said:

"We both like sex and I haven't had any since you know when. How about a friends with benefits relationship? Or forget the friends and do a neighbors with benefits. What do you think?"

I thought about it most of the night and part of the morning. Shari was damned good in the bedroom and …. Suddenly I woke up to what I was thinking, shook my head to clear it and muttered "Fuck no!" I made a mental note to call Gloria when I got back from camping and then I reached over and turned the radio back on and listened to Toby Keith sing about how much he liked a bar.

The End

Here is a sample from another story you may enjoy:

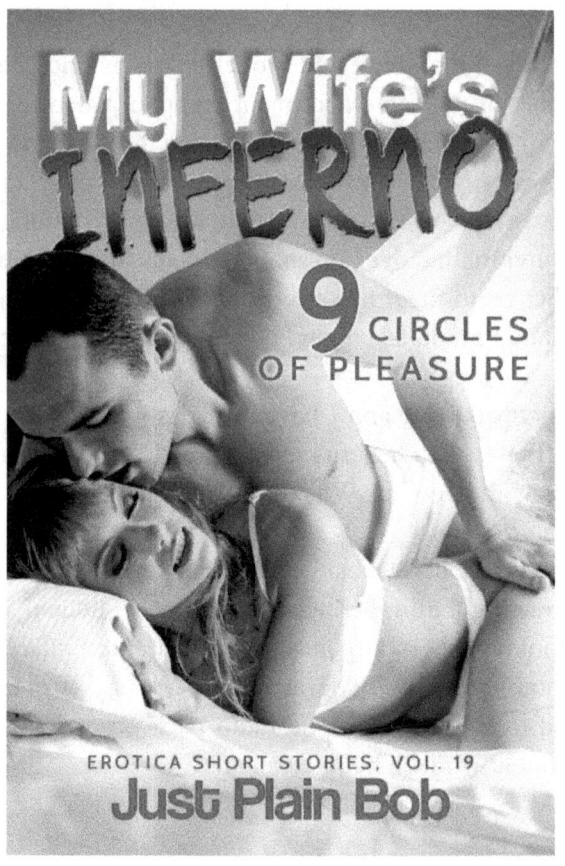

My Wife's INFERNO

9 CIRCLES OF PLEASURE

EROTICA SHORT STORIES, VOL. 19
Just Plain Bob

It was just another boring cocktail party until she walked in. I saw her look around with a "Why in the hell am I here" look on her face and then our eyes met. I'll swear to my dying day that a spark jumped between us.

She made her way toward the makeshift bar and I excused myself from the group I'd been talking with and headed for her. I moved next to her at the bar and before she had a chance to order herself a drink I said:

"You don't want to be here any more than I do. May I suggest that we leave and go someplace where we can get to know each other?"

I saw the smile behind the cool, appraising glance she gave me and then she said, "Do you have any place in particular in mind?"

"Well, it is too soon in our relationship to ask your place or mine, so I was thinking about some place close by. Maybe Mario's? They make a killer martini there and it's just around the corner."

Over martinis I learned that her name was Fiona, that she was twenty-seven years old and that she made her living as a painter of portraits, still-lifes and landscapes. When I asked her if there were any men in her life she looked me right in the eye and said, "Not until now."

"Does this mean that it's time for the your place or mine question?"

"How close are we to your place?"

"Fifteen minutes."

She reached for her purse, "Mine's only five – let's go."

Following her to her place I wondered what was happening to me. I've chased a lot of ladies in my time and I've been successful with quite a few, but it was never like this. Never had I looked at one and knew - just knew - that she was the one that was meant for me. And never, not ever, had things moved so quickly. From opening conversation to leaving Mario's it was less than forty-five minutes. I wondered if she too had felt the spark or whether she was just easy.

It did not take me long to find out that she was perfect for me. She unlocked the door of her apartment and was taking off her clothes before I was even inside. She pulled me toward the bedroom.

"Hurry, come on, hurry."

There was no foreplay - we hit the bed and went after each other like two people possessed and it was perfect. I instinctively knew what she wanted, where and how to touch, and she knew the same about me. The only way to describe it would be to say we fit - we were made for each other. After the first frenzied fuck she brought me back to life with the best head I'd ever gotten. Our second coupling, while not as frenzied as the first, was still intense and when it was over I surprised her by going down on her cum filled pussy. She told me later that no man had ever done that to her before. We went twice more before falling asleep wrapped up in each other's arms.

I woke to find her leaning on an elbow and looking down at me. When she saw that I was awake she said, "Will I see you again or was I wrong in thinking that something special happened between us last night?"

"I felt it, but I didn't know if you did."

"Oh I felt it all right."

We did not leave her bed until six that evening and only then because we needed something to eat besides each other. After eating we went to my apartment so I could get a change of clothes, but we were no sooner in the door than she asked me where the bedroom was. I pointed and she headed for it stripping as she walked. I had more sex that weekend than I'd had in the previous two months and I was pretty much exhausted when I dropped her off at her apartment on Sunday night. As she got out of the car she said:

"Are you sure you won't come up?"

"If I come up I'm liable to miss work tomorrow."

She laughed, "Yeah, you probably would."

"I get off work at five."

"I'm sorry baby, but I'm busy tomorrow night. How about Tuesday?"

I told her that I would see her then and I headed on home.

For the next three months Fiona and I saw each other every night but Monday and Thursday. When I asked why I couldn't see her on those days she told me that those were the two nights when people sat for portraits. I told her that I'd love to watch her work, but she said no.

"You would be too much of a distraction for me baby, and I couldn't afford to be throwing down my brushes to rip off a quick piece."

It was something that I could understand so I didn't press her on it.

At the end of three months I proposed. Given the way we felt about each other I expected the proposal to be a slam-dunk so I was stunned when Fiona said no.

"But why not? We are perfect for each other."

"I won't marry you because I don't want to give up my independence. What we have is working and I don't see any need to change things."

I worked on her for another two weeks, but she wouldn't budge on the matter. I finally decided to drop the matter before I ended up screwing up what we already had.

Another three months went by and one day I was having a business lunch with a client and I saw Fiona walk into the restaurant on the arm of a man I didn't know.

Frank saw where I was looking and he smiled and said, "She really is a looker, isn't she? I wish I had the price."

If you enjoyed this sample then look for **My Wife's Inferno**.

Also by this Author:

The Prodigal Family: The Abbotts

Watching My Shared Wife

The Waitress and the Runaway Husband

Baiting Mr. Little

Too Hot for Henry

Chuck's Fantasy

The Redhead's Desires

Rescued at Riley's

His Every Fantasy

Open Mike Night

Pursuit for Revenge

Why Does He Do That?

Halloween & Drugs

Tracey

When Rob Met Kari

Becoming a Shared Wife, Vol. 1 –

(Wife Sharing and Other Adventures)

Becoming a Shared Wife, Vol. 2 –

(Hazardous Wives)

Becoming a Shared Wife, Vol. 3 –

(Wives Who Stray)

He was ten minutes late. He stood on the doorstep, mortified.

Luis apologised profusely. "I am so sorry, Jan," he said, almost wringing his hands with sincerity. "I hate being late for my clients. I *hate* it," he hissed with Latin fervour.

Jan waved his protestations away. "Don't worry, Luis. It isn't as though I've signed up yet, is it. I'm not a proper client."

"Even more reason I should not be late, Jan." He shrugged and pulled a face, finally taking in the incongruity. "I ... uhm…" Luis began, blinking in surprise. He pointed to Jan's feet. "I don't think you should wear those for training, Jan."

Luis's late arrival gave Jan the excuse she needed. "Oh, the Jimmy Choos?" she said, then lifted one foot. Jan examined the decorative tassels adorning suede straps, the shoes featuring a metal and suede chain that fastened around the ankle. "A shimmering leopard print at the back of the shoe," she informed a clueless Luis. "4.7 inch heels *might* be a little dangerous," Jan conceded with a smirk. "But I was just trying them on. I thought I'd have a little time. They were a gift from my husband. What do you think?"

Still standing at the front door, Luis glanced over Jan's shoulder. "Your husband is home?"

Shaking her head, Jan replied with, "Oh, no, Luis. No-no-no. He's away overseas on business." She offered the man a smile. "Won't you come in?"

Blinking again, Luis followed Jan into the house, his eyes taking in the odd yet extremely pleasing sight of a shapely woman in a tight leotard cut high on her hips who was also wearing high heels.

"I, uh, think those shoes are very nice, Jan," he said as Jan led him along the corridor.

"Thank you, Luis," the woman replied. "This is my little gym," she introduced with a flourish when she opened the door. "I hope you can show me how all the…" Jan paused on a sigh and non-too-subtly added, "…*equipment* works."

It took some effort for Luis to drag his eyes away from that lascivious smirk. But he eventually managed it, somehow contriving to appear interested in the fitness apparatus.

"What--" he gurgled, clearing his throat of the bird's nest lodged there before continuing. "What do you hope to achieve, Jan?"

Luis desperately tried to avoid the woman's intense and very disturbing gaze.

This wasn't a first for the trainer. He'd experienced the come-on before, and – so far – resisted the seductive advances of horny females.

But this one … *this* one, with her big round tits, fantastic legs, sly smile and those fucking shoes…

She had the edge on the others, and Luis was so tempted to re-linquish his proud professionalism and succumb to her obvious desire.

He stepped further into the room, following Jan, her heels giving off a hollow thunk-thunk against the parquet flooring when she moved.

Jan sat astride the rowing machine, back straight, impressive frontage thrust forward.

"I think I'm in good shape already," she said, throwing a mean-ingful look at Luis. "But I'd like to tone up a bit. My arms, my tummy and legs…

"I want to look good when I go out, Luis. I want men … *young* men to look at me."

Jan's voice dropped to a husky murmur that settled a blanket of anticipation over them both.

"I want gorgeous young men to look at me, and I want them to want me."

Luis gulped, boggling at Jan. His mouth opened and closed a few time until he finally blurted, "But, what about your husband?"

"What about him?" Jan replied, shrugging one shoulder. Then she just came out with it. "How about I suck your cock?"

Luis succumbed, with the straightforward question so abruptly delivered robbing him of the capacity to think. He couldn't formulate a response in time, and before he knew it, Jan had yanked at the elastic waist of his tracksuit bottoms and brought his cock bouncing out, the thing already halfway to an erection.

His penis stiffened considerably when Jan's fist cranked at it, her gasp and subsequent murmur of appreciation aiding its swift growth.

"Oh, God," Jan breathed, her habitual breathless response during sex. She was doing it. This was it; her first adventure planned and executed; her first deliberate cuckolding of Charles.

Jan didn't count Paul as deliberate. In Jan's mind their sexual liaison was a residual effect of what had happened in the workshop, the result of her carnal epiphany.

"I hope I've got condoms big enough for you," the woman breathed, eyes fixed on the tumescent length.

She eased Luis closer by squeezing his cock and gently pulling him round as she swivelled at the waist. Next, Jan jacked Luis's erection several times, threw a glance up to register the shocked expression on his face, and then took him between her lips.

Luis moaned, fingers pushing into Jan's short hair as he tried to take a handful in his grip.

"Jan…" the man mumbled, the sounds of her slurping coming up to taunt him. "Ah, fuck…"

"Mmm," Jan responded, cheeks concave.

She held Luis's cock fast with her mouth while easing the lycra skin of the leotard around the outer flanks of her breasts. Then Jan massaged her boobs and allowed the thick erection to spring from her lips, the thing disengaging with a distinctly juicy plop.

Then she rose to her feet to offer her tits to her lover.

The sight of the distended nipples, Jan's teats long and thick in the coins of their areolae, inflamed the young man, and any doubts about giving Jan what she wanted evaporated along with concerns about her marital status.

Luis grabbed breast-flesh, squeezing against pliant resistance while simultaneously moaning and bending to suck a nipple.

Jan lifted the man's head from her breast, bending at the waist so she could paint her nipples with the slippery cock head, smirking at him before she pouted, eyes glazing.

The look he gave her in response sent an arterial burst of flaming desire through Jan, the feeling so intense she squeaked and then groaned when Luis kissed her mouth.

"You want this?" the man growled, emboldened with lust. "Eh? Is it, Jan?"

"Let me get a condom," Jan replied when Luis waggled his cock with one hand. "I can't wait. I want to fuck."

If you enjoyed this sample then look for **Making Him Watch**.

***

DEXTER'S
Renaissance

LEE NORTH

Hot Romance Erotica

That May picnic was the beginning of a series of dates that Michelle and I enjoyed. Sometimes to a movie or play, often for dinner, occasionally for a ballgame. It was on one of those dates that there was a distinct shift in our relationship. Until then, we had held hands, kissed lightly, and generally behaved ourselves. I think we both could feel the pressure building. It changed after we had spent a pleasant evening at a local play.

We were in her late model Lincoln and I was driving. In the past, I would stop at the Rossmoor and she would drive on to her apartment. That night she had other ideas.

"Drive to my place, Dex. It's Friday, and we've got all weekend. You haven't been to my place yet and I'd like to spend some time with you," she said, placing her hand over mine.

It didn't take me any time at all to agree and head toward Lakeshore Drive. As we neared the building, Michelle took a small transmitter from her purse and pushed a button. The open grilled gate began to rise and I drove into the underground parking area as she directed me to her numbered space. The transmitter also unlocked the door to the elevator and stairs. After waiting a moment for an available car, a door slid open and we entered with Michelle inserting a card and pushing a button marked "R."

When we stepped out of the car, a large glass window was directly in front of us and I could see we were at the top of the building. To the left was 2102 and to the right, 2101. Michelle guided me right and opened the door, stepping in and turning on some lights.

It was a very nice and apparently large penthouse suite, one of two on the top floor of the building. As I looked around I saw the trappings of affluence; fine furniture, interesting artwork, and lush carpeting.

Michelle kicked off her shoes and I followed suit.

"Dex, I'm all sticky from the humidity today. I'm going to have a shower and change. Why don't you do the same, then we can relax and get to know each other better," she smiled.

I wasn't about to decline the offer and happily agreed. She led me to the main bathroom, handed me some towels and a washcloth and told me how to work the controls on the shower system. I needed the lesson. It was a multi-head system with pre-selected temperatures. The cabinet itself was almost as big as the bathroom in my apartment.

As I soaped and rinsed, I almost expected that Michelle would suddenly appear and join me, but that didn't happen. I stepped out of the shower, towelled myself off, and dressed in my slacks and shirt. I didn't bother with socks. They wouldn't be as fresh as I was so I stuffed them in my back pocket as I headed barefoot for the living area.

Waiting for Michelle, I wandered about the spacious penthouse. There was a dining area with a very nice buffet and china cabinet, along with a large period-style table and chairs. The kitchen was through a wide passage and it too was large, with a big island and plenty of cabinet and counter space. Most houses didn't have this much room.

I was just coming out of my inspection of the kitchen when Michelle reappeared and got my undivided attention. She was wearing a black silk pyjama suit, if that's what it's called. It was floor length, very sleek with material flowing from its wide legs and arms. She had a smile for me as she approached, then stopped and swirled in a circle to emphasize the graceful lines of her attire.

"You like?" she asked, already knowing my answer.

"Very nice … very elegant." I almost added very sexy. As she had moved to show off the garment it was immediately apparent that she was wearing nothing beneath it. Her nipples protruded clearly in front and her buttocks were perfectly outlined in back. I could feel my erection beginning to develop.

"Would you care for coffee ... or perhaps a glass of wine or brandy?" she asked in a tempting tone.

"I'd like a glass of brandy, please."

"Oh, good. I'll have one too," she said, turning to move into the kitchen.

I followed her as if she was drawing me along. Perhaps it was the magnetic appeal of her, dressed as she was in such alluring garb. She reached up in a cupboard for the brandy bottle and I stepped behind her to help her. I was directly behind her now, touching her slightly with my hips and chest. On the spur of the moment, I did something I would never have thought I would do.

With the fingertips of my right hand, I lightly, slowly, ran them up her side, feeling her ribs as I went. Then, in a moment of complete recklessness, I moved my hand and gently cupped and stroked a fulsome breast. I felt her shiver from the contact but she didn't push me away or resist my touch. In fact, I was sure I heard a soft moan.

I couldn't see her face, but she had begun to lean back into me, the brandy bottle now forgotten. Her hands were on the countertop as if bracing her against an assault. My left hand joined the right in teasing her nipples and now her groan was more audible. Emboldened, I allowed my left hand to slip down over her abdomen and softly rub the silky smooth material of her gown.

I felt her backside push slowly back into me and she could certainly now feel my erection. I moved my hips to place my hardened member between her cheeks. She welcomed that with a swaying motion that only reinforced my hardness. One of us was going to have to do something soon.

It was Michelle who took my right hand and guided it inside her top, giving me access to her breasts. She pulled at the fold of the material and I felt a little pop as a small snap released the upper half of the garment. Still holding my hand, she slid it down to her waist where another small snap gave way and the gown parted completely.

I felt her shrug her shoulders and the lovely black item fell at her feet. She was naked before me, still facing away but leaning back more urgently against me, pressing herself into my prominent manhood. Once more, I did something I would not have thought I could attempt. I intimated with my knee that I wanted her to spread her legs and she immediately complied. She understood exactly what I was intending.

I unbuttoned my pants and they too fell at my feet, my briefs following them almost immediately. I took my cock in my hand and began to stroke her already wet centre in preparation for my entry. Again, she did everything she could to help me and within a few moments I was pushing into her. Slowly and carefully at first, but her insistence gave me courage to thrust a little more and soon I was buried well inside her.

I moved a little more forcefully and quickly as she continued to encourage me. There was absolutely no doubt in my mind that this was what she had planned all along. Her voice soon joined the action, not so much with words but with little cries of encouragement and pleasure. How long it had been since she had been with a man I did not know. I only knew she was with me now, and I was reaping the reward of her pent up need.

I leaned my head forward and captured an earlobe between my lips, then licked the back of her neck as I continued to stroke into her. In response, she threw her head back, growling a pagan, earthy moan of lust, slamming her ass back into me, the smacking sound of our joining now growing louder. This was probably going to end quite soon, but I did whatever I could to hold off as long as possible.

A few moments later her moves became more erratic and we almost fell out of rhythm as she began her orgasmic journey. I stayed with her as long as I could, but I was going to finish as well and there was nothing I could do to prevent it. I felt myself release into her once, twice, then a third time. As I did, she sagged against me and I wrapped my arms around her waist so that she didn't collapse against the granite counter or on the floor.

In all my experience, limited as it might have been, I had never had a more erotic, spontaneous coupling than this. I was in no condition to continue. Michelle was leaning back into me, breathing heavily and holding my arms tightly as they encircled her. Not a word had passed between us from the time she walked to the liquor cupboard.

I'm still not sure what got into me that night. I was either very confident of myself or very reckless. Probably the latter. Nonetheless, I picked the naked beauty up in my arms and carefully steered my way out of the kitchen toward the master bedroom. When I arrived, I saw that the bed had been turned down and I carefully laid Michelle on it crosswise with her legs dangling over the side. Her eyes were open and she was staring at me, no doubt wondering what I was doing. Still, neither of us had yet spoken.

I pulled off my shirt and now as naked as she, I got on my knees on the lushly carpeted floor, my hands gently but insistently pushing her legs apart. Again, she offered no resistance. I moved between her thighs and began to kiss the flawless, smooth skin. I was about to work my way up to the place where I had just planted my seed when I felt her hands in my hair. Was this a 'stop' or a 'go?'

I could see a bit of my semen on the lips of her vagina and I wondered what possessed me to try this. What was I trying to prove? Yet, even with that question in my head, I continued. As Michelle realized what I was planning, she must have had second thoughts. That had prompted her to place her hands on my head again, trying to decide if she should put a stop to my intentions. As I made up my mind to continue, I felt her resistance lessen.

I moved toward my target and slowly, with the flat of my tongue, I began to make love to her once again. This was going to be a very different kind of penetration. I had plenty of experience with oral sex but none just after I had planted my seed inside a woman. It was too late to stop now, and Michelle was making no sign that she wanted me to.

In fact, I was bringing her back to life with my tongue and fingers. Her hips were rising and falling erratically, responding to whatever stimuli she felt. Her grip on my head tightened and I could feel her fingers in my hair. She was holding on tight, her body dancing to whatever music my tongue created. I flicked the tip of her clitoris and got the response I expected. Her hips snapped up in reaction.

I was beginning to tire … or at least my tongue was. Michelle was nearing another orgasm and I willed myself to continue. At last she let go and I could stop and rest. I crawled up beside her, lying on my back. She rolled over me and gave me a deep, soulful kiss. Whatever I had accomplished, she approved of it. I wondered if it was something her late husband had not provided.

We lay there for a while, her head on my shoulder, our legs dangling over the edge of the bed. I kissed her forehead and ran my fingers through her soft, flowing hair. Her hand was holding my now flaccid cock, not manipulating it, just holding it lightly.

"That was wonderful," she said at last. "I didn't realize just how much I wanted you and you were perfect for me."

"We took some chances tonight," I said. "That gown didn't leave much to the imagination."

"It was either that or I would just come out naked. It was a coin toss."

"Were you worried I wouldn't get the message?"

"That thought did cross my mind. I can never be sure just what you are thinking about when it comes to women, Dex. Sometimes shy, but tonight a completely different person. You took command and I was the lucky one when you did."

"You were irresistible. I'm sure that was your plan, wasn't it? Well, it worked. I couldn't resist you, so everything that happened was a result of that."

"You'll stay tonight, won't you?"

"Yes. You might regret it in the morning, but I do want to stay. I want to wake up with you."

"We've started something, haven't we?" It was as much a statement as a question.

"I hope so. Is that what you want?" I wondered.

"Yes. As little as I know about you, as little time as I've known you, everything I've learned tells me that you are right for me."

"Well, we're going to have some time to find out so let's enjoy ourselves and see where it goes. I'm not a one-night-stand kind of guy. I'm looking for something more than that."

"You wouldn't be in this apartment tonight if I thought otherwise. But now that you're here, I'm going to keep you here as long as I can."

After a few minutes, Michelle rose and padded to the ensuite bathroom, closing the door behind her. She returned a minute or so later and crawled on top of me, rubbing my still limp cock with her lightly haired sex. I began to respond to her tantalizing little game and she noticed.

"Oh … isn't that nice. Can I have some more please, sir?"

"Of course you may. Just tell me your heart's desire, young lady, and I'll try and fulfill your wishes."

"Well, after that glorious fucking you gave me in the kitchen, I think I'd like you to make love to me. Something nice and slow and lasting."

"How would you like me to start? A little foreplay, perhaps?"

"I think I've had all the foreplay I can handle tonight, Dex. I'm still carrying some of you around in me and what I really want is to have you inside me again."

If you enjoyed this sample then look for **Dexter's Renaissance**.

***

It was 10:35pm when I let Victoria into my suite. Chloe was hiding in the bedroom closet with the hand held video camera all ready to record the evening events. April was hiding behind the kitchen counter that was out of view from anywhere in the suite unless you went directly into the kitchen area. She had the second burner cell phone that the video would be copied on from the camera that Chloe would be using. Jenny was underneath the bed in the bedroom with a very small but powerful audio microphone so we could record every word that would come out of Victoria's mouth.

"You are so gorgeous, Victoria," I announced as we came in the door. "I'm flattered that you want to do this with me." That was the cue to start the video and audio recording. "I bet that there have been many men that have wanted to have you," I stated coyly. Victoria was beside herself with pride as she told me that she has fucked three professors, two football coaches and the starting 12 offensive players of the football team.

"I can't believe that three professors would risk their positions for a one time chance with you." Without hesitation, Victoria blurted out their names. Then she even told me exactly WHEN the hook ups occurred and the name of the hotels that they used. "You must be really good in bed for those three old men to risk their jobs and marriage for." I chuckled inside as I stroked her pride. "But I still find it hard to believe that two coaches would have time away from their busy schedule to bang you," I teased her. She again named the coaches as well as where it happened and exactly when. "Wow, you really have been a busy girl," I smiled broadly. "But how on Earth did you manage to fuck the entire starting twelve football players?" I coaxed as I pushed her back onto the bed. "They paid me to have a party with them," she announced proudly as I pulled off her heels and began to remove my shirt. "You mean...they PAID you to fuck them?" I made my voice sound incredulous. Victoria had her eyes glued to the bulge in my shorts as I dropped my pants and kicked them off.

"Oh Yes, they did," she moaned as I pushed my shorts down to expose my throbbing prick. "They rented a fancy suite like this and took turns coming to the bedroom to fuck me," she nearly moaned it as she stared at my cock. "They each gave me $100 after they fucked me and they all said I was the best fuck they ever had," she told me triumphantly.

"And it was fourteen if you count the punter and placekicker," she added with a giggle.

I now had all the damning information that I would need to end her threats. From this point forward I would use her as my plaything and punish her for her attempt to blackmail me. "Roll on your tummy, baby...I'd like to take a look at that gorgeous ass," I told her softly. Once she was on her stomach, I pulled the zipper down on the side of her skirt then ripped it all the way down till her skirt came apart and fell off. I yanked it out from under her and threw it on the floor.

"Do you enjoy reading my stories," I asked her softly while I gently fondled her gorgeous ass cheeks. "Oooh Yes Jake, I've been reading your stories since I was a little girl," she gasped as I slid my hand between her legs to finger her gash gently. "I used to steal them from my mother and...Play with my cunny while I read them in my room," she confided with a soft moan as I pressed a finger up into her dripping snatch. "Oooh Jake," she purred.

"Have you ever noticed that the main character in my dirty books loves to fuck his hookers up the ass?" I pressed my thumb straight up her ass when I said it. Her body was vibrating as I rammed my fingers and thumb in and out of both her holes. "Have you noticed that he loves to pull out and urinate all over those whores when he's done?" I growled in her ear as I bent forward. "Is that what you want? You want to be MY whore like you were for those boys? You want me to fuck you up the ass and piss all over you?" I bit on her earlobe after I finished whispering in her ear.

"No Jake...Please...I just want this...to be special. Just this once." Her entire body was writhing on the bed as I continued to shove my fingers in and out of her pussy and ass. SLAP...the force of my smack on her ass cheek left a glowing red imprint. "Okay, roll over and spread those legs for me then," I groused as I yanked my fingers out of her.

I ripped her blouse open as soon as she was flat on her back. "Did you enjoy fucking those fourteen boys," I growled as I slipped my dick up into her drenched slit. "Oooh Yes Jake. Yes," she groaned. "When you get paid to fuck that makes you a whore." I pulled my dick out then slammed it back in. "Are you MY whore Victoria?" Her body shuddered. "Oh Yes Jake, Yes I am," she groaned. I could feel the gush of her arousal as she shuddered again. As I humped my dick into her I sucked two hickeys onto her neck and then three more on her left tit.

Smack, Smack, Smack, Smack...as I slammed into her as hard as I could, I raised up with my arms to gaze at her pinned beneath me. Her tits jiggled and her body bounced on the bed as I pounded into her over and over. "Tell me you are MY whore," I grunted as I felt the orgasm building up in my nuts. "Tell my girls...you are my whore," I shouted. "YES JAKE, I'M A WHORE, I AM YOUR WHORE," she screamed as her body jerked into climax. I yanked my dick out of her and scooted forward so I could spray my load of cum all over her face and chest.

If you enjoyed this sample then look for **Take Three, Mr. Writer.**

WANT FREE COPIES OF MY BOOKS?

Just visit my blog and download free copies of my books:

awesomeauthors.org/justplainbob